THE LAST DOMINO

THE LAST DOMINO

adam meyer

G. P. PUTNAM'S SONS

NEW YORK

G. P. PUTNAM'S SONS
A division of Penguin Young Readers Group
Published by The Penguin Group
Penguin Group (USA) Inc., 375 Hudson Street, New York, NY 10014, U.S.A.
Penguin Group (Canada), 10 Alcorn Avenue, Toronto, Ontario, Canada M4V 3B2
(a division of Pearson Penguin Canada Inc.).
Penguin Books Ltd, 80 Strand, London WC2R 0RL, England.
Penguin Ireland, 25 St. Stephen's Green, Dublin 2, Ireland (a division of Penguin Books Ltd.).
Penguin Group (Australia), 250 Camberwell Road, Camberwell, Victoria 3124, Australia
(a division of Pearson Australia Group Pty Ltd).
Penguin Books India Pvt Ltd, 11 Community Centre, Panchsheel Park, New Delhi—110 017, India.
Penguin Group (NZ), Cnr Airborne and Rosedale Roads, Albany, Auckland 1310, New Zealand
(a division of Pearson New Zealand Ltd).
Penguin Books (South Africa) (Pty) Ltd, 24 Sturdee Avenue, Rosebank, Johannesburg 2196, South Africa.
Penguin Books Ltd, Registered Offices: 80 Strand, London WC2R 0RL, England.

Designed by Gina DiMassi. Text set in Aldus Roman.
Library of Congress Cataloging-in-Publication Data
Meyer, Adam, 1972– The last domino / Adam Meyer. p. cm. Summary: Vulnerable following
his brother's suicide, a high school boy comes under the thrall of a darkly violent classmate
and events at home and at school go chillingly out of control.   [1. School shootings—Fiction.
2. Murder—Fiction. 3. Family problems—Fiction. 4. High schools—Fiction. 5. Schools—Fiction.]
I. Title. PZ7.M56797Las 2005   [Fic]—dc22   2004015626
ISBN 0-399-24332-1
10 9 8 7 6 5 4 3 2 1
First Impression

for meghan, who knows

MANY, MANY THANKS TO my parents, to Scott and Karen, and to my family. Also thanks to my friends, both in and out of the TV trenches. Among them, Robin "Schnapps" Samuels, Cheryl Torrontor, Roger Angle, Tori Hartman, Eva Batonne, Chris "Cobbler" Stanton, and John Carlson bravely read and commented on this novel at various stages—I'm grateful they did. Rob Tiger and Peter Toye deserve mention for sheer longevity of friendship. And on the research front, Marilyn Howard put a gun in my hands, and Gareth Howard showed me what to do with it.

Barbara Solowey, Tom Piccirilli, Bruce Harris, Tim Coleman, Karl Edward Wagner, John Douglass, Brian Leonard, Rebecca Campany, Robin Sestero, Alison Picard, Frank Scatoni, and Lawrence Block helped make me a better writer—and LeRoy Hudson, Daniel Saltzman and John Whalen reminded me why I write. This book wouldn't exist without them.

Finally, thank you to my wife, Meghan, who believed in this book from the beginning, to my agent, Jennifer De Chiara, who changed my life with an extraordinary leap of faith, and to my editor, Susan Kochan, who always asked the right questions.

THE LAST DOMINO

I RODE MY DEAD BROTHER'S bike down the concrete path that split the main lawn of Shadwell High. I felt like I was being watched by the stone lions on either side of the front steps. The cement was uneven beneath my tires, and every time I hit a bump the gun in my waistband jabbed my lower back.

I cut off the path and followed the grass to the bleachers, my legs still sore from the beating P.J. had given me. Pedaling on the lawn was harder than on the concrete, but I kept going.

I settled on the lowest bench, spreading my backpack open. Everything I touched was full of memory and regret: a sketch of my friend Daniel being crushed by a desk, some half-finished pencil drawings of Koryn, a root beer can with a bullet hole, and a trophy with WORLD'S GREATEST BROTHER stamped on a cheap metal plaque. But I reached past those things and found a folded-up piece of paper that said LIST OF PEOPLE WHO NEED TO BE SHOT.

I ran my fingers across the names that filled the soft, worn paper and tore it up into tiny pieces, sprinkling them in the grass. Guess I should've put my name on there first, I thought, and reached under my shirt for the Beretta.

I slid my fingers around the grip and put the barrel in my mouth. There was a lump in my throat as big as a bowling ball and a kick in my chest like the back legs of a mule. I shut my eyes and flexed my finger in the trigger guard, clamping my teeth so hard my gums ached. This was it, the moment I'd been waiting for, the chance to be just like Richie.

I imagined my brother in this same spot six years earlier. My hand shook and a tear squeezed out of my eye. Pain blossomed inside my head and I knew there was only one way to cut it out.

Pull the trigger.

But I couldn't. I felt hopeless and useless, which was how I always ended up. But this time there was more. I felt angry and determined too, and I could do something about it, because I had all the power in the world clenched right between my fingers.

With a growing sense of purpose, I spit out the taste of gunmetal and slid the Beretta into my bag. I walked toward the school, holding my backpack so close that I felt my heart racing. As I reached for the front door and glanced back at the bleachers, I saw Richie's bike on the grass with its front tire sticking up.

I went inside, knowing I'd never ride the bike again.

THE VOICE

ON THE FIRST DAY of my junior year, I threw open the front door and charged down the hall, sneakers skidding on the polished floor. I wanted only one thing: to get to first period before P.J. Riley.

I knew he was going to be in English with me, because he'd grilled me on my schedule a few weeks ago at Coffee Time. And I had just leaped to first place on his shit list, all because I threw a rock that bounced off the windshield of his Taurus.

I'd planned to get to school early, but now it was only three minutes until the bell. Thanks to my mother's constant delays—first she didn't know where the hairbrush was, and then her car keys—I was way late. I hoped P.J. was too. I ran down the hall to the stairs and flung the door open. My breath flew in and out, my stomach flopping around like a fish in a bucket. Whispers chased me.

"You hear about Travis?"

"He must be whack, just like his brother."

"They say he was trying to off somebody with those rocks."

That's not what happened, I wanted to shout, but I knew no one would listen. Besides, there was no time.

I raced up the first flight, leaping up the steps two at a time. But as I hit the second-floor landing, I came to a screaming stop. A couple blocked my way, making out against the tile wall. The guy's face was hidden behind a curtain of girl-hair. A strip of tanned skin showed between her jeans and T-shirt.

I cleared my throat so they would know I was there, but it still took them a second to pull apart. When they did, the guy—Jordan Beaumont, it turned out—said, "Hey Travis." He had straight sandy hair and a slightly crooked smile that made all the girls go crazy. Thanks to a blown-out knee, he wasn't on the football team anymore but he still had the cred of an athlete. Although we'd worked together at Coffee Time all summer, we almost never talked.

Amy Hasselman spun around in front of him, Jordan's old football jacket hanging off her narrow shoulders. "Jordan, ignore him," she said. "He's crazy."

"Relax, Ame."

"But he tried to kill P.J."

"It was an accident."

"He's right," I said as Amy flattened herself against the wall so that I could pass. But I just stood there, staring at her.

Back in grade school she'd been short and fat and unpopular, and sometimes she'd eaten lunch with me and my best friends, Moira and Ross Lansbury. Amy and I used to hang out at the annual IBM company picnics too, since both our fathers worked there. That stopped when we were in middle school, about the time Richie died. This had more to do with Amy than with Richie since that's when she started shedding her baby fat and sprouted breasts.

"Just go away," she said now, looking at me like a chunk of dirt on a white rug.

Why doesn't she *just go away, right, Trav-oh?*

My body stiffened, arms as straight as telephone poles. Where had those words come from? This didn't feel like a thought from my own head, more like something that had invaded my brain. And there was only one person who'd ever called me Trav-oh.

I had no time to think about it though. Unsettled, I squeezed past Jordan and Amy and climbed the rest of the steps.

I ran down the hall, and finally reached 339. Inside the room, I spotted several familiar but not friendly faces—Lee Kartinski, Missy Relling, Sean Delaney, Tiffany Erstad. And there, worst of all, was P.J.

There was only one person I didn't know, a kid in a loose Hawaiian shirt and baggy cargo pants. He stood with Mrs. Saxon, who looked the same as she had last September and the September before, her heavy body topped with a puffy face and her thick dark hair held back by a wooden barrette.

"Mr. Ellroy," she said. "How nice of you to join us."

Around the room, people let out chuckles between their fingers. I was the only person Mrs. Saxon ever called by his last name. Like a lot of my teachers, she'd had my older brother as a student and used to call me Richie by mistake. This way she didn't have to worry.

You'd think she could remember me though, since I'd had her for three years already. I always sat in the same place too, the last seat in the back row against the wall. But as I went for my spot, I saw a blue backpack flopped there like a beached whale, and knew there was only one person who would've done that. The new kid. He hovered by Mrs. Saxon's desk, hands in his pockets, hair dripping over his face. He was a little taller than me but he didn't look any stronger.

I had a sudden vision of myself grabbing his backpack and hurling it across the room, his pencils and notebook spewing out all over. The new kid would turn to me with surprise and horror as I snatched his desk—*my* desk—and lifted it high overhead. You want it? I'd scream. Take it.

But I couldn't do that. I just stood there and looked for another place to sit. There was an empty desk next to P.J. and another in the back, beside my usual spot.

I wasn't going to sit near P.J., of course, and I headed back along the far wall so that I could avoid him. But he was still only two rows in, and all he had to do was look past the empty desk beside him and he'd see me.

I avoided his eyes as I approached, counting the steps it would take to get past him—seven, six, five . . . To my surprise, he didn't

7

even blink as I walked by. But just as I took my next step, eyes locked on the desk I wanted, I heard him say, "You," and my stomach dropped.

P.J. generally looked bigger sitting than standing, since most of his size was in his chest, and he always squinted, like he needed glasses. Maybe that's why he sat only three rows from the board, instead of further back like most other athletes.

"You got my three hundred bones yet?" he asked.

"Not yet," I said.

"Not yet?" P.J. said, mimicking me. "How long am I supposed to go around with a cracked windshield?"

"I don't know," I said.

"You'd better come up with a better answer than that."

I've got an answer for you. Why don't you shove those three hundred bones up his ass?

There was the voice again. This time I was sure of two things: it wasn't random and it was *real*. These words were mine somehow, though they came from a place I'd never known about. That frightened me more than anything, even the look that P.J. had screwed onto his face.

Fighting back a shudder, I thought of the hill above Route 9, where I had stood a week ago with two pockets full of stones. I'd found them at the edge of the creek near my house. They were about the size and weight of the golf balls my father putted in the backyard.

When I got to the top of the hill, I was surprised by the strength of my first throw. I'd never had an arm like Richie, but as I arched forward and shifted my weight, the rock soared high over the treetops. It landed in the road, just inside the white line.

I threw twenty more rocks and most went at least that far. A few of the rocks landed on cars, and one even cracked the windshield of a black Taurus. Unfortunately, the Taurus was P.J.'s, and P.J. was the football team's star running back, not to mention Sheriff Eugene Riley's son.

Fifteen minutes later, Sheriff Riley and two deputies climbed the hill toward me. Watching the men move in, panic unrolled inside me. I realized that the whole time I'd been throwing rocks I wasn't afraid—not of being caught, not of what my parents would say, not of the sheriff or anything.

Sheriff Riley took me to the police station and asked the same questions over and over. I gave the same answers and eventually that seemed to satisfy him, except there was one question he wouldn't give up on: *Why?*

"Why the hell did you do it?" he asked, again and again. I gave him the almost-honest answer—"I don't know"—every single time. Finally he accepted it as the truth.

When my parents showed up, the sheriff went on a long tirade about how I could have killed someone out there, then finally he said he wouldn't press charges as long as I paid to fix P.J.'s windshield. My parents agreed to that condition before I even had a chance to speak.

It was only a week since then and I had just sixty bucks saved up for P.J. I'd begged my parents to loan me the rest, but my father said I had to earn it. In the meantime, I was at P.J.'s mercy.

"Are you going to stand there all day?" he asked, watching me with his beady eyes.

Before I could answer Jordan strolled in, fingering a spot of lipstick on his neck. As P.J. turned to slap hands with him, I bolted for the empty seat in the back of the room. Across from me, Missy Relling—a math nerd with delusions of popularity—twirled her pencil around a piece of hair. "Aw, can't have your favorite spot," she said. "You're not going to throw any rocks at me, are you?"

I half wanted my newfound voice to pipe up. It didn't, and I just sat there.

"God, you're so pathetic, Travis." She was about to say more, but the new kid was coming toward us and something in his face stopped her. Maybe it was his sense of calm or else it was his eyes, which looked as flat and glassy as a bird's.

He sat beside me and said, "Hey, I'm Daniel Pulver."

I shrugged and turned to the front. As Mrs. Saxon droned on about attendance procedures and late penalties, she looked pointedly at me. I pretended to listen until she turned away.

I looked back at Daniel, but he was writing in his notebook, so I let my gaze settle on Koryn Walker. She was two aisles to my left and three rows ahead. She'd drawn a few strands of her thick brown hair into a single green braid that hung over her shoulder. She wore loose purple pants and a tight white shirt. Although she dressed and acted different than everyone else, people rarely made fun of her. It was probably because—weird clothes or not—she was the prettiest girl in school.

When Koryn turned I looked away quickly and flipped open my own notebook. Instead of making the usual pictures of comic book characters like the Collector or Magneto, I started sketching a figure more like me: eyes and nose too big for his head, hair combed to the side, a T-shirt over baggy jeans. Then I did reality one better, giving myself arms and legs knotted with muscles. With a few more pencil strokes I added an overturned desk high over my alter ego's head.

The bloody mess sprawled below him might have been anyone, but as I filled in details—a tropical shirt, sloppy hair—this character's identity was clear. I had begun to outline the jagged crack in his skull when a slip of paper landed on my desk. I was about to pass the note on to whoever it was for when I saw my name in block letters. Inside, two words in spiky print jumped out.

KILLER DRAWING.

Despite the note, Daniel Pulver pretended to study the blackboard, one hand cupping his chin. What a prick, I thought, but there was a warm feeling in my gut. I was angry that he'd been spying on me. But I was flattered too.

Crumpling his note, I laid an arm across my notebook and continued to draw furiously. I worked the pencil back and forth, again and again, finally pressing so hard that the tip broke. As I reached into my backpack for another, the end of period bell rang.

"Before you go, everybody take one of these." Mrs. Saxon waved a copy of *Wuthering Heights* and pointed to the stack on her desk, then stepped out into the hall.

I held out my drawing for Daniel to see, but he was already on his way to the front and didn't look back. Asshole, I thought, smoothing out his note. I wanted to chase him, but I'd learned my lesson: I wasn't going anywhere until P.J. was gone.

Koryn was the first to reach the pile of books. Missy Relling followed, flipping through copies to find the one she liked best. Daniel Pulver took the first book he touched, and others followed. Finally Jordan and P.J. grabbed books and headed for the doorway, playpunching each other the whole way.

When I got to the front, all the decent-looking copies were gone. I grabbed a dog-eared one and flipped it open. There were a ton of pages, and the print was tiny. Great.

As I tucked the book under my arm, P.J. looked in from the doorway. I nearly jumped. He held up three fingers and mouthed the words "three hundred," then dropped all but the middle finger and smiled. In the time it took me to fumble *Wuthering Heights* into my backpack and pull the zipper, he was gone. Hot tears stung my eyes, and suddenly I was glad to be alone.

New York State Police
interview with Koryn Walker

DET. UPSHAW: So you knew Travis ever since you moved to Shadwell in ... eighth grade, wasn't it?

KORYN: Yes.

DET. UPSHAW: But you'd never had a relationship with him until your junior year?

KORYN: We never had a relationship, Detective.

DET. UPSHAW: I understand. What I mean is, a friendship. You were friends, weren't you?

KORYN: For a little while, I guess so. Yes.

DET. UPSHAW: Did you initiate that friendship or did he?

KORYN: I don't know. It just sort of happened.

DET. UPSHAW: It happened when you started working at Coffee Time?

KORYN: Yes.

DET. UPSHAW: At the time had you heard about Travis being picked up by the police?

KORYN: Of course. Everyone knew, everyone was talking about it.

DET. UPSHAW: Did that concern you, knowing he'd thrown rocks at passing cars?

KORYN: Not really. It sounded like some stupid thing, a mistake that had gotten blown out of proportion. Travis wasn't the kind of person who wanted to hurt people ... that's not how I saw him.

DET. UPSHAW: How did you see him?

KORYN: I ... he seemed really sweet. He was funny too. And he was so shy. I guess hardly anyone was nice to him. And

I thought maybe if I was nice that ... never mind. It
doesn't matter.

DET. UPSHAW: Please, I'd like to know. You thought that if
you were nice, what?

KORYN: I thought that maybe he would ... maybe I could ... I
really did like him. (SOUNDS OF CRYING) Oh God. Oh God, how
could I be so stupid. ...

WHEN I LEFT SCHOOL that afternoon, I felt like the only person in the world who wasn't going off to have fun. Some kids drifted to the parking lot, buzzing about their afternoon plans, while others filed onto the bus, exchanging slips of paper with e-mail addresses and cell phone numbers. I ignored all of them, going out the front gate to South Main Street.

From behind me, I heard a voice: "Hey! Where you going?"

Turning, I saw Moira Lansbury waving her arms at me like she was flagging down a rescue plane. Her brother Ross stood beside her, hands in his pockets.

"To work," I said, drifting back to meet them.

"That sucks," Moira said.

"Tell me about it."

Although Ross and Moira were twins, the only thing similar about them was their bright blue backpacks. Moira was an inch taller than me and about thirty pounds heavier, though she always tried to hide her weight with baggy sweaters. Ross was short like me but skinnier, his shirts and pants always hanging off him. Like their parents, Moira had dark hair, skin, and eyes, while Ross was blond and fair with green eyes. Moira sometimes joked that Ross was adopted, but he never laughed.

"Can't you get out of work?" Moira said.

"Not really."

She didn't push any further. She knew I needed the money, and she knew why too.

"Come over after," Ross said. "I've got this cool new game and—"

"Ross, c'mon!" Moira had turned and started running back toward the bus, which had just closed its doors. She waved her arms again, even more frantically this time, and ran at full speed, her fleshy arms jiggling. Through the bus windows I saw people laugh at her. I looked away.

"I'll see you tomorrow!" I called out, but not very loudly.

I took my time walking through town. I remembered when I was four or five, playing on the sidewalk with Richie while Mom was in Klean Right or Schwamlein's Pharmacy. We'd run up and down like crazy, although Richie—seven years older—always yelled if I got too close to the curb.

Passing the tinted windows of Tiger's Pub on the corner of South Main and Broadway, I had another memory. I was eleven and my mother and I were driving back from Little League practice. I was catching imaginary fly balls in the passenger seat when I saw him in the pub doorway. "There's Richie," I shouted, waving.

"Where?" my mother asked.

"There, right there," I said, pointing as the door closed on him.

My mother stepped on the gas, roaring too fast down Main. "That wasn't your brother." Her tone of voice warned me not to argue, so I didn't, but I knew. I'd wanted to ask what it was like to go in a bar, but I didn't think of it again until a month later. By then Richie was dead.

Coffee Time was on the far side of Broadway. There were a few cars in the lot but no one in line and just a couple of girls from Bard College lounging at the fake marble tables. Toby Danzig, a Bard student herself, was behind the counter as I came around, watching me with eyes as big and black as eight balls.

"Good thing you're here," she said. "Gus is in rare form."

"Where is he?"

"In the crapper."

15

I went into the back room and pulled my wadded-up green apron out of my backpack. I'd already changed into my uniform—khaki pants and a white shirt—after seventh-period gym. I was tying my apron on when I noticed a flyer pinned to the bulletin board above the desk.

SHIFT SUPERVISOR WANTED.

There was a list of qualifications: someone who had worked at least two hundred hours in a Coffee Time franchise, had a good knowledge of products and procedures, and was willing to learn new tasks. But forget the job. I was stuck on the money—"up to eight dollars an hour"—which was a big jump from the $5.50 I was making. At that rate, I could pay off P.J.'s broken windshield almost twice as fast, and any cash after that would be free and clear.

I leaned in to study the flyer some more when Gus slammed through the swinging doors. Although he was twenty-four, Gus didn't look much older than the kids in school. He liked to remind us that he was "the youngest store manager in the region," and he didn't hide the fact that he was determined to be a regional director by twenty-six.

"You're late again," he said in his grumpy employee voice. His face was so smooth you could see the point of his chin. "We need you out there."

I could've replied that the store was almost empty, but I had the promotion on my mind.

"We've got that new girl starting at four," he added. "So let's make sure we're caught up before she gets here."

I was anxious to ask about the shift supervisor job, but figured I'd wait. Still, I felt high with possibilities.

When Toby clocked out a few minutes later, there was little to do, so Gus told me to sweep up. Normally, I could stretch a job like that for half an hour, but in fifteen minutes I had the floor so clean even my father couldn't have found a speck of dirt on it. "Do you want me to wipe off the pastry cases?" I asked, leaning on the broom.

Gus looked suspicious. "Sure, do that. And fill the cream and milk too."

While I sprayed glass cleaner on the display cases, Gus told every customer how excited he was about the new Mountain Blend or invited them to try one of his lattes. I shifted to the condiment bar, pouring milk from a gallon jug into one of the metal pitchers. I kept thinking about the promotion. I saw myself wearing the brown shift supervisor's apron, ordering Toby and Jordan around.

The thought made me smile, but the smile crumpled as I spilled a stream of milk over the top of the pitcher. It spewed onto the condiment bar, seeping onto the packets of sugar and Sweet 'N Low. Some even splashed on my pants and drizzled on the tile floor.

"Travis, for crying out loud!" Gus shrieked.

I jumped back from the growing puddle and nearly collided with someone. Turning, I found myself looking at Koryn Walker.

"Jeez, Travis, I'm sorry."

"Not your fault," I mumbled, studying her. She was even prettier up close, her cheeks as smooth as fine china, gray eyes so faint they were almost silver. Her dark hair fanned out across her shoulders, the green braid trailing behind her ear like the vine of a rosebush.

Gus glanced at a sheet of paper on his way over. "You must be Koryn," he said, using his customer-voice, not his employee one. "And it sounds like you know Travis."

"From school," she said.

"Travis, clean up this mess while we go over a few things," Gus said. "You think you can at least manage that?"

As Gus led Koryn away, I got on my knees and laid out a wad of towels. I felt like the biggest loser who'd ever lived, and I was sure my new coworker would have to agree.

After Gus took Koryn through the start-up paperwork and gave her an apron, they spent about five minutes at the register before he checked his watch. "I've got to submit the new bean orders or we're going to have to start selling tea and tap water. Travis, can you help me out?"

"Huh?" I'd been idly wiping the counter. My pants were still damp with milk and I wished I could go home and change.

"Just give Koryn the rundown on the register and the different drinks. Okay?"

Koryn watched Gus strut toward the back room. She stood with one hand on her hip and the other on the register's touch screen. She'd changed into a white Polo shirt. "This looks complicated," she said, frowning.

"It's not," I said. "Um, basically there's . . . there's your, um, coffee of the day, cappuccino, latte, and mocha."

I took a deep breath before going on. "Gus won't admit it, but you only sell these other foofy drinks maybe once or twice a week." Koryn looked pleased, as if I'd shared a secret. "And when you're calling the orders out to the drink bar, you've got to remember to say it the right way."

"Okay," Koryn said. "So if somebody wants, I don't know, an iced skim cappuccino, uh, medium—"

"No, see, you've got to call it like this—medium skim iced cappuccino."

Koryn nodded, repeating the words to herself.

"There's something that might help," I said, and realized too late that I should've kept my mouth shut. It was a saying Toby had told me when I was first training there.

"Well?" Koryn asked, raising her eyebrows.

"Well, it . . . it's kind of rude."

"I'm sure I can handle it, Travis."

I breathed deep and started talking. "The drink order's supposed to be SMTD—size, milk, temperature, drink." Lowering my voice to a whisper, I said, "Or, well . . . Suck My Tasty D—"

Koryn's laugh cut me off, and I was grateful. But I wasn't sure if she was laughing at me or with me.

"Well, I won't forget that one," she said, smiling. I barely felt the wet spots on my clothes anymore.

After that I let Koryn ring up the orders. Though I could find the buttons faster, she was more at ease with people than me. "How are you folks doing today? . . . Oh, I really love your jacket, now what can I get for you? . . . A cappuccino, great." And when she called out the drinks, she even used the right order.

Finally we had a lull. Koryn looked at the coffee grinding machine behind us, then said, "So what do you usually drink here?"

"I, um . . . I just drink whatever." The truth was if I got thirsty, I usually just had water. I hated coffee. "What about you?"

"Usually I just get milk with vanilla syrup." Lowering her voice, she added, "I don't really like coffee. I only took the job here because it's closer than the mall."

My heart started to race. "Me too."

"You don't like—"

"It's gross."

Koryn was about to respond when a battered black Taurus streaked across the parking lot, a green Mustang on its tail. The Taurus had a blue and white bumper sticker on the front fender that read

SHADWELL SHARKS, and next to that P.J. had scrawled KICK ASS. There was a white spot on the windshield about the size of a quarter. A jagged line extended out from the small circle like a scar, and through it I saw P.J.'s meaty face.

P.J. and his girlfriend Taffy got out of his car, and Amy and Jordan climbed out of the Mustang. Jordan came through the door first, his apron in his free hand. P.J. followed, his face still streaked with black chalk from football practice, with Amy and Taffy behind him.

Amy wore the team jacket she'd had on earlier, although the sleeves were pulled down now over her long fingers. She was small compared to P.J., but Taffy was even smaller, looking like an oversized doll in her see-through blouse over a tank top and jeans.

Taffy had been one of the popular kids since kindergarten and though we were never friends, we did have a strange sort of bond. The summer before Richie went away to college, our dog Simms— as in Phil, Richie's favorite quarterback—was hit by a car. When we brought him to the vet, Taffy was in the waiting room with a black poodle. Dr. Carelli took Richie and Simms in the back and I started crying. Taffy came over, her poodle sniffing around her heels as she put an arm across my shoulders.

After a few minutes Richie came out and said it was time to go home. Taffy pulled away and I followed Richie. On the ride home, I kept asking about Simms, but all he would say was, "It's better this way, Travis."

I'd never said anything to Taffy about what happened at the vet's office, not even "thank you." I looked at her now, wondering if I should wave or something, but she didn't notice me. Only Jordan did.

"Things been busy, Travis?" he asked.

"We've got it under control."

"I hope you're working hard," P.J. said, looking pleased to discover me there. "I mean, I know you need the cash. *My* cash."

As P.J. crept closer to the register, he noticed the stain on my pants. A smile creased his lips. "Hey, you should've told us about your accident. We would've brought diapers."

Amy stifled a giggle. "Come on, you know big kids like Travis use Depends."

P.J. laughed and Taffy half smiled. Jordan's face was hidden as he pulled his apron over his head. Koryn frowned. I turned away, shoulders hunched like a turtle's, my pleasant buzz slipping away.

If those pricks are such comedians, why don't you give them something to laugh about, Trav-oh?

It was the voice again. Its words wafted through my guts like smoke from a forest fire.

Leave me alone, I thought, but I didn't know if I meant the voice or the group across the counter. Before I had a chance to think about it, Gus swooped out of the back room. "You're here," he said, smiling at Jordan. "I want to talk about, you know, what we talked about yesterday."

"Okay, because I—"

"Later." Gus looked from Amy to Taffy, his gaze barely rising above their chests. "Good to see you again, ladies. Um, Travis, why don't you take off a little early today?"

"That's okay," I said, glancing at Koryn. It was the first time ever I hadn't jumped at the chance to get out of there. "I don't mind—"

"Clock out, all right?"

As I punched my employee code into the computer in back, I saw a pile of blank shift supervisor forms beside it. Despite the milk incident, I still felt like I'd earned some points with Gus, so I filled out an application and left it on top of the pile.

Leaving the back room, I saw Taffy and Amy beyond the plate glass window, each hanging on one of P.J.'s broad shoulders.

I trailed behind the counter, watching as Jordan held a pitcher of

21

milk under the steamer wand and waved out the window. Koryn studied him from behind, and I felt a stab of jealousy as hot as fresh coffee. Outside, the Taurus's tires shrieked as it peeled away. The sounds helped cover my escape, and I was only inches from the front door when Koryn said, "Travis."

I turned.

"I'll see you tomorrow," she said.

"I'm not working tomorrow."

"Oh, me either." When she smiled, the white of her teeth was dazzling. "I meant in English class."

I replayed her words in my mind as I pushed out to the parking lot and put my hands deep in my pockets. I didn't want Koryn to see them shaking.

I guess I haven't written here since I got off my crutches. Seven months now. Sometimes it feels like yesterday. Or like a million years ago.

Not sure why I'm even doing this. Writing, I mean. Like I told Mom when she got me this, diaries are for girls. "But it's a journal," she said. "Guys can keep journals too. Your father used to have one, you know."

Actually, I didn't know that, or at least I don't remember. But I was tired of playing video games and reading horror novels, anyway. Couldn't do much else with my bad knee.

Knee's fine now, of course. Well, not fine, but good enough for walking. Just like I walked by the football field this afternoon. Saw P.J. and Schlong and Ted out there. Doing stuff I used to do.

Maybe I won't think about football so much now. Especially not with Amy around again. I picked her up for school an hour early. We drove out to Old Post Road. The sun was coming up. We macked for a while, then did stuff.

She kept saying, "I missed you."

We had a good time in the car and in the hallway. And after school, behind the bleachers. But here's the thing—I didn't miss her that much. Not like I should've after two months. I spent a lot of time alone this summer. Just driving and thinking. And I liked it. But then I got tired of being alone, wished Amy was around. Now she is, and I feel the same.

But I haven't even mentioned the big news. My promotion to shift supervisor.

Gus says it's got to stay our secret until next week. He has to interview a couple people for looks, then do some paperwork. Amy's psyched. I should be too. And I am. Still, I wish I'd been able to say, "Sorry. Too busy with football."

Almost forgot the other thing that happened. Had to work with Koryn. She's one of those crunchy types, listens to all this weird music. Parents are professors at Bard. Total hippy chick.

I was showing her how to make a cup of espresso and she went, "Is that your car?" Looking at my Mustang.

"Yeah."

"Be great for a road trip. You could just go wherever."

"Like an explorer," I said.

Her eyebrows went up. Maybe she thought I was kidding.

"I love old explorers, guys like Lewis and Clark and Magellan and Columbus," I said. "And I kind of had this idea of going around someday and seeing different cities. Take a few pictures, send some postcards. At least say I'd been there, or somewhere."

"So when do we leave?" She had a funny smile. But her voice was serious.

"Well, I'd have to say good-bye to a couple of friends."

"You'd better decide where we're going first. Unless you want me to do it."

"Huh?"

"Even if we play it by ear, we've got to have someplace to get us started."

Which is a pretty weird thing to say. But then she's a pretty weird girl.

15 DAYS TO GO

ON MY WAY TO LUNCH that Tuesday I stopped in the library to look at the yearbooks. The walls were plastered with portraits of famous authors carefully painted by Mrs. Vinto, the old librarian. Over in the reference section, Edgar Allan Poe, Charles Dickens, and Jane Austen glared at me. As imagined by Mrs. Vinto, they all looked a little constipated, especially Poe.

I stood at a wooden shelf between one of the tall windows and Poe, hearing the hiss of Principal McCarthy going "shhh." He did that about every five or ten seconds, whether anyone was making noise or not. Mrs. Vinto had died of a stroke when I was a freshman, and ever since then Principal McCarthy and a few of the English teachers took turns covering the library.

As I knelt down to the bottom shelf, my fingers traced the rough edges of the yearbooks. Sunlight spread across the faded gold letters on the spines. I looked for the 1997 edition. I liked flipping the pages of it and studying the faces I'd seen at birthday parties and football games, but my favorite part was the student wills. I'd been through the book so many times, it was never hard to find Richie's.

But as I scanned the yearbooks from the nineties, I found an unexpected gap. My fingers pushed at the space between 1996 and 1998 like a tongue probing the spot where a tooth was pulled.

The one for 1997 was gone.

"Are you finding what you need, Travis?" asked Principal McCarthy.

Standing, I shrugged. "Just looking at the yearbooks," I said. "But there's one missing."

"I hope no one stole the book, Travis. These yearbooks are very

25

valuable to the school. Priceless, even, you might say. And we can't
have students just walking off with them."

I couldn't believe what I was hearing. "I didn't steal it," I said.

"I'm not saying you did."

But he was, I knew that from the tone of his voice and the look
in his eyes. Anger bubbled up inside me as I glanced at Poe, the
writer's lips pushed together as though he were trying to shit a brick.
I imagined grabbing the canvas from the wall and smashing it over
Principal McCarthy's head. Steal this, I'd shout, as I shoved him in
the gut and knocked him through the tall window.

"I'll let you know if the yearbook turns up," he said.

"Thanks," I muttered, hurrying out of the library before he could
stop me.

My pulse throbbed as I made my way down the hall. Why would
Principal McCarthy think I stole the yearbook? What if he called
my parents about it? I was in enough trouble with them already.

I hurried down the first-floor hallway. There was a side exit behind me and straight ahead at the far end of the hall was the cafeteria. The main entrance was down another hall off to the right, with
the series of school offices—including Principal McCarthy's—
starting where the two halls formed a right angle.

I had just reached that spot when a woman stepped out of the
guidance office, tall and thin though not as skinny as I remembered.
Beth Kittinger's auburn hair barely curled past the collar of her silk
blouse. I'd liked it better when her hair was long and spread onto her
shoulders like a bundle of summer straw.

"Travis," she said, smiling. For a moment I saw her as she'd
looked in the old days, long tan legs in denim shorts, face glistening
with summer sweat. Still Richie's Beth, I thought, though her knee-
length gray skirt and plain leather shoes made her look very adult.

"I've been keeping an eye out for you," she said. "How are your parents?"

"Oh, they're the same."

"And how're you?" The scent of her perfume was faint but noticeable, making me think of the time I'd come in from the backyard and spotted Beth and Richie side by side on the basement sofa. They didn't notice me as I listened to the quiet sounds they made, their hands disappearing into each other's shorts. I went into the basement a lot after that, but I never caught them like that again.

"I'm fine," I said.

"It's been a long time, huh?"

"Yeah."

"Well, you'll be seeing plenty of me now. My office is right there." She pointed at the doorway behind her. "I hope you'll come see me sometime. It doesn't have to be official. Just, well, if you need someone to talk to."

There had been a lot of talking the year after Richie died, when Beth used to come around once a month for coffee with my mom and dad. I liked to sit with them, though I never said much. They started with small talk but quickly turned to old stories about Richie: Do you remember the time he dressed up like a clown for his birthday? How about when he brought home the stray dog that chewed up the sofa? Oh, but the best was after those kids sprayed graffiti outside Mr. Barth's store, and Richie rounded up half the senior class to repaint it, only it was bright yellow and Mr. Barth had a fit.

The time between visits kept growing longer and longer until Beth stopped coming at all. That was three years ago and I hadn't seen her since.

"You know I have one of the pictures you drew for me when you were little," Beth said. "Daffy Duck, I think. Do you still draw?"

As I started to answer, Koryn and her friend Laurel Zito went by. Laurel whispered to Koryn, who tucked her green braid over her shoulder. As they passed, I fought the urge to lean over and try to listen to what they said.

"Sometimes," I said. "I've got to go."

"Okay. I'll see you later then."

Turning away, I saw a page from the yearbook as clearly as though it was in front of me: RICHIE ELLROY'S LAST WILL AND TESTAMENT—*To Beth, I leave a hug and a kiss and a promise that I will always be there for you, unless it's Super Bowl Sunday. To my parents, I leave my last game-winning touchdown. And to Trav-oh, who will be in high school soon, I leave this advice—don't do anything I wouldn't do.*

Ah, I thought, Beth must have taken the yearbook from the library. She was the only person, besides me, who'd want it. But why hadn't she told Principal McCarthy? When I turned to ask her, she was already halfway down the hall.

"Who's that?" Moira asked through a mouthful of salami, nodding toward the far end of the cafeteria.

"Who's who?" I replied, half turning. At first I just saw P.J. and Jordan arm wrestling across one of the tables. Although P.J. was stronger and heavier, his arm was only a few inches off the table.

Around them, Amy and Taffy were comparing nail polish while their friends cheered. There was Ted Burnitz, who'd used his size fourteen cleats to earn a perfect record as a football kicker; Gil "Schlong" Schlom, the backup quarterback who'd embraced his nickname; and Gil's cheerleader girlfriend, Dana La Bret, who wore more makeup than all the other girls in school combined.

"That guy over there," Moira said.

Daniel Pulver sat three tables away, picking quietly at the food on his tray. Like me, he had bought the school meal of burnt lasagna and cold green beans. Unlike me, he ate alone.

"That's the new kid," Ross said, pushing a piece of his own salami sandwich between his lips.

"Well, duh," Moira said. "But who *is* he?"

I'd noticed Moira watching Daniel during lunch the day before, but she hadn't said anything then. She was cautious about approaching new people, so something about him must have appealed to her.

P.J. had started to overwhelm Jordan, the muscle curving out from P.J.'s arm like half a tennis ball. Squeezing his eyes down to slits, P.J. grunted again.

"I think he's Daniel something," I said, although I knew his name perfectly well. I still had the note he'd passed me, along with the drawing I'd made of me and him. "He's in my English class."

"Maybe he's nice," Moira said. "It can't hurt to find out."

"Yes it can," I said.

Moira scowled at me. Whatever she did she was persistent about it, and I knew from the way that she tapped her fingers that she wasn't going to give up on this. I felt an unexpected twinge of jealousy. What if Moira and Ross got to know Daniel and ended up liking him better than me, and they all ate lunch together while I sat off by myself?

"Let's at least find out more about him," I said. "Make sure he's not a dweeb."

"Yeah, like you," Ross said.

Across the cafeteria, P.J. closed in on victory. Jordan's arm was only six inches off the table. Cords stood out on the side of his neck, but he wasn't giving in. Amy layered polish on her nails, one eye on her hand and the other on Jordan. Taffy looked past them, studying her own nails, but there was a sparkle of interest in her eyes.

Calling on some hidden strength, Jordan's arm started to rise, one inch, then two, and I thought he might be able to overtake P.J. But P.J. let out a grunt that rose steadily in pitch and slammed Jordan's hand down to the table.

As the rest of the table cheered, P.J. held up his arms like a boxer who'd scored a knockout, while Jordan shook his wrist out. Amy, who was still painting her nails, leaned her head against his shoulder. I looked away before they could notice me watching and held my breath, half expecting P.J. to come over and demand that I arm wrestle him next. But he didn't challenge me, and neither did Moira. At least not yet.

New York State Police
interview with Moira Lansbury

DET. UPSHAW: Would you say that Travis was your
best friend?

MOIRA: My best friend and Ross's too. Sometimes I even
thought of Travis more like a little brother than a
friend. I mean, he wasn't really younger but ... I guess I
can be kind of bossy sometimes. And ever since Travis's
real brother ... oh, forget it, I shouldn't.

DET. UPSHAW: Tell me, Moira. Please.

MOIRA: It's just that Travis changed after his brother
Richie killed himself. It was like, he was always a little
bit sad, even when he was happy. But I got used to that, I
guess, after a few years. Of course he changed again,
when he met Daniel. But that's one change I never did get
used to.

DET. UPSHAW: How did Travis change this time?

MOIRA: Oh, I don't know. Travis always used to be really
quiet and sweet, just a good person basically. And I know
that he still hurt about Richie, and he was angry at the
way his parents treated him, and he hated getting picked
on at school. But Daniel got in there and kept reminding
him about the ways he hurt. It was awful, like poking a
stick in someone's eye. And everyone says it's Travis's
fault, what happened, but it's not, not totally. Because if
Daniel hadn't come along ... I don't know. I just
don't know.

ON FRIDAY NIGHT I SAT down at the kitchen table with a plate of mashed potatoes and meat loaf and flicked the remote at the TV. Nothing happened, so I pushed the power button a couple more times. Zilch.

The television used to be Richie's, and I was surprised my mother hadn't locked it away in his old room with everything else of his. We'd never watched TV at dinner when he was around. We didn't have to. My brother would spend half the meal going on about football practice or yearbook staff meetings or some road trip he and Beth had taken. After he died, the only sounds were forks clinking against plates. Then one day my father set up Richie's TV behind his empty chair. Suddenly our kitchen was filled with voices and laughter, and even if it wasn't ours, it was better than silence.

Tonight, however, the screen was blank. When the remote's power button still didn't work, I figured the batteries were dead. But as I walked to the TV to turn it on, my mother said simply, "Don't bother. I unplugged it."

My mother, Eleanor Ellroy, was small and awkward with Richie's straight black hair and something of his nose. Overall people said she looked more like me than my brother, but she never could see it herself.

"This should be family time, and we're a family," my mother said, as reasonably as if she were quoting interest rates. She worked as a loan officer at the Key Bank in downtown Shadwell, but she'd always dreamed of being a dancer. She still took ballet classes in the basement of the Episcopal Church on Wednesday nights. "The TV's just a nuisance, a distraction, and I won't have it squawking at us anymore."

I wanted to shout back at her: Watching TV is my chance to see what a normal family is like! But I stayed silent, shrugging as if I didn't care.

"Your mother's right," my father said, opening a bottle of Heineken. His voice was too loud, as if he were trying to be heard over the sound of a show that wasn't on. "We don't really need it."

"Well maybe I do," I said, looking for the plug.

"Sit down, Travis. When your mother tells you something, you'd better start listening." He poured beer into a tall glass, gathering his thoughts. "I don't know about 'family time,' but I do know this—we need a little discipline around here. People are going to have to do what they're told when they're told."

By "people" I knew he meant me, so I sat and stared at him. His suit was spotless, his white shirt starched. The only times I'd ever seen him messy he'd had a smudge of dirt on his cuff or a speck of grass on his knee after a game of golf. He'd given up golf the winter before, after his back surgery, and now he only played on his computer or in the backyard.

"Are you doing this because of the rock throwing?" I asked, voice sharp with anger.

"We're doing this for *us*," my mother said. "You've unleashed a cry for help, a plea to be noticed, and I want you to know that we hear your message loud and clear. Thanks to Dr. Hawke, I see how much we've drifted apart, and I want to pull us together. Like a family." My mother took a deep breath, as if she were about to dive into a pool. "Now Travis, tell us about your day."

I wondered if abruptly changing the subject was one of Dr. Hawke's strategies for family bonding. He was the therapist my mother had started seeing. She wanted me to go too, but I refused and so had my father.

"My day sucked," I said.

"Travis, that's not nice."

"Well, it's true."

"Oh." My mother looked troubled and then her eyes brightened, as if someone had flipped a switch inside her. "Well, I had a wonderful day. This morning I helped a lovely young couple apply for their first mortgage, and later I ran into Maggie Beaumont. You're still in school with her son Jordie, aren't you?"

No one had called him Jordie since kindergarten, but I said nothing, just stirred my mashed potatoes. They were as thick as old paste.

"Jordan's on the football team, right?" My father sounded more comfortable discussing sports, but that third beer probably helped. "What I hear, they've got a great squad this year."

"Jordan hurt his knee last season," I said. "He doesn't play anymore."

Smiling, my mother said, "Even if he did play, I'm sure the team wouldn't be as good as when Richie was around."

I heard what sounded like a gong, but it was only my father slamming his fork down on his plate. The urge to scream rose clear from my toes to the roots of my hair.

"What?" My mother turned up her hands. "I'm not supposed to mention my son?"

"Your son's right here," my father said.

"In case you've forgotten, Thomas, I have two."

"*Had*, Eleanor. Richie's dead, and I don't want to hear his name spoken at this table again. Do you understand me?"

"Well you're the one who—"

"Are you listening or not?"

My mother fumed silently for a moment, then fired back. "I won't keep burying the past. I can't. I want to heal, I want all of us to heal, and we can't do that unless we talk and remember and—"

"I can remember plenty, thank you," my father said. "But I'm not going to keep living in the past. And I won't put Travis through this constant rehashing, either."

"It's not rehashing, it's making peace. There's a difference."

"The hell there is. That stupid quack has you so goddamn brainwashed you can't even tell the difference between your ideas and his."

"Now that's not fair."

They went on like that as if I weren't in the room. I felt my skin tighten around the bones of my face and squeezed my fork so hard it hurt.

Oh yeah, this is some family time. Just what Dr. Hawke had in mind, don't you think, Trav-oh?

The sound of the voice loosened one of the knots in my gut.

"I'm not going to pretend that Richie wasn't a part of this family," my mother said. "By embracing his memory, by accepting our past, we can better focus on the future."

My father shook his head. "Don't give me any more psychobabble bullshit, okay, Eleanor?"

"No, I'll just give you another goddamn beer."

I looked at the reflection of my parents in the blank TV screen, their faces twisted like images in a fun house mirror. Turning to the clock, I willed the hands to jump ahead to seven, when Ross and Moira were going to pick me up.

I was desperate for some way to change the tone of the dinner conversation, and searched for something to say but couldn't find it. Then I remembered standing in the woods over by Route 9, full of the reckless power of hurling stones over the treetops, not knowing where they would land or what would happen next, and maybe that's why I jumped in and said: "By the way, I'm getting a promotion."

Both my parents turned at once. My mother's eyes flickered with surprise, and my father's were dull but warm.

"At work?" she asked.

"Yeah, from clerk to shift supervisor."

"Why didn't you say anything before?" my father asked.

I shrugged, as though I were being modest.

"Are you going to have to work extra hours?" my mother chimed in. "Your grades might start to slip. I mean, you're not the student Richie was."

My father shot her a warning glance but said nothing. I felt a splinter of anger pierce my calm, but that didn't stop me from going on.

"It's okay—same hours, more money." I grinned, amazed that I could keep up the lie.

Suddenly the mood at the table was different. My father chewed with satisfaction and my mother looked at me as though I had changed somehow. And maybe I had. I imagined coming home from my first day as shift supervisor wearing my new brown apron, getting a big hug from my mother and a firm handshake from my father. They would ask me where I wanted to go to celebrate and I'd suggest Foster's in Rhinebeck, the fanciest place I knew. We'd only been there once, after Richie was named MVP of the state championship game.

I heard the muffled sound of a car horn. Backing away from the table, I said, "That's Ross and Moira."

When I got up, my father held out a crisp new twenty. "Go ahead," he said, mistaking my surprise for hesitation. "Consider it an advance on your promotion."

I closed my palm around the bill and savored the warmth in my father's eyes. "Thanks."

As I went to my bedroom to grab my jacket, I paused at the door across from the bathroom. It was almost two weeks now since I'd stood there with the key in the knob, ready to go in.

It all started in mid-summer, when I was looking for an old shoe to blow up with some firecrackers. I went rummaging through my mother's closet, a place I never really went. As I dug through scuffed pumps and torn sneakers, I saw a key hanging on a nail against the wall. It was strung on a piece of blue ribbon, like the ribbon on the citizenship medal Richie won in eleventh grade.

Over the next three weeks, I opened the closet a dozen times, putting the key in Richie's door twice. But it wasn't until the Sunday before school started that I decided to use it. My father and I were watching football on TV, Bills and Patriots, when the New England quarterback picked up a fumble and ran like a demon, going seventy yards for a touchdown.

"Wow-eee, you don't see that every day," the announcer marveled. But my father and I must have had the same thought: we'd seen Richie do it in a county championship game.

I said, "You remember that?" but the look on my father's face—soft in the flesh but hard in the eyes—stopped me. He flicked off the TV and said, "Oh, were you still watching?"

Then he vanished into the master bedroom. After a couple of minutes, I turned the TV back on and flipped channels, turning the volume up loud on some Clint Eastwood western. When I saw my father reappear in his golf clothes and stumble to the back door, I went straight for my mother's closet.

A minute later I stood at Richie's door and turned the key. Over the sound of blaring violin music from the TV, I hadn't heard my father come back. He'd probably forgotten his lucky socks, or maybe he knew in his bones what I was about to do. Whatever it was, he saw me there.

"You stay the hell out of Richie's room," he said, trembling. "Don't you have any goddamn sense? That's private, and we don't go in there. Do you hear me, dammit? *Do you?*"

Whatever he saw in my face—defiance, hurt, or maybe simply confusion—it infuriated him, his whole body quivering with anger. His hand rose and he slapped me, fingers cracking across my chin, and I was so surprised I couldn't move. My father had never hit me, not even when I was a little kid. I stared at him, dumbfounded, and he stared back.

Turning, I ran out of the house and kept on running until I reached the creek, where I found the smoothest, roundest stones and gathered them into my pockets until my pants were so heavy I could barely walk.

The next thing I knew I was on a hill, launching rocks at the road below.

A couple days later, when I had gotten up the courage to look in my mother's closet again, the key was gone.

The Lansburys' SUV hunkered at the curb, exhaust curling from the tailpipe like dragon's breath. Moira waved from the driver's seat. Ross breathed circles of fog on the passenger window. The SUV's back windows were tinted, so it wasn't until I yanked on the door that I saw my friends weren't alone.

Daniel Pulver wore another Hawaiian shirt, this time with yellow and white flowers. His face looked different than it had in school, less pale but more focused.

"Hey," I said coolly as I got in. I nodded at Ross, then glared at Moira, and pretended Daniel wasn't there at all.

Moira chattered on and on about this new video game they'd

picked up. "We've got all the best stuff." She searched the rearview mirror for my eyes. "Don't we, Travis?"

"Pretty much, yeah." She and Ross had every gadget known to mankind: video games and tons of movies and computer stuff. Ross loved to use it all, but I always felt Moira enjoyed having it more than using it.

"You could come over tomorrow," Ross said. "Both of you guys."

I didn't like what I was hearing. I spent most weekends at the Lansburys', anyway, since it was better than being at home. But we were fine as a threesome. We didn't need Daniel or anyone else.

Fortunately Daniel said, "I can't. My grandmother's in the hospital and my mom's making me go see her."

"Well, sure, she's your grandmother," Ross said.

"That sucks," I said, fighting back a smile. It was wrong to be glad about something like that, but I was.

"That's okay, Danny," Moira said. "Another time."

"Maybe, but there's one thing. My name's not Danny, not Dan, not D. It's Daniel." He paused, looking straight at me. "Nicknames are for dorks."

As we pulled into the mall parking lot, I thought about how Richie used to call me Trav-oh. But he was the only one who'd ever done it and there was no way Daniel could know that. Still, I felt his eyes going through me, although when I looked over he was turned to the window, not aware of me at all.

The tension seemed to lift as we went through the mall together. We talked about seeing a movie, but instead we looked at clothes and music and books, then hit the food court, where we gorged on beef meximelts and huge drinks. Instead of soda Daniel called it "pop," which I claimed was the funniest thing I'd ever heard, and I laughed so hard *pop* sprayed out of my nostrils and onto my shirt.

As we ate, I told everyone about the promotion coming up at

Coffee Time and how I really hoped I would get it. I felt guilty about my parents, but only a little.

"I'm sure you'll get it," Ross said.

"Just don't get your hopes up," Moira warned.

"He's the best worker there," Ross said.

When we compared notes on our new classes, I complained about having Mrs. Saxon for English again. "She's just so boring," I said.

"She's worse than boring," Daniel said. "She's an obnoxious cow who treats her students like imbeciles. I can't stand her."

"I had Mrs. Saxon last year and she was okay," Moira said.

"She's not okay. I hate her and I hate all those stupid kids who suck up to her and I hate the whole goddamn school. It's not like we really learn anything that matters, anyway. Do we?"

Moira looked at Daniel as if trying to decide whether he was serious. Ross, who hated to disagree with anyone except for Moira, shrugged cryptically. I just sat there, even as I heard the voice.

He's right. All you learn in school is how to be a good little robot. Do you really want to be a robot, Trav-oh?

I didn't reply, to Daniel or to myself. But he kept looking at me as if waiting for me to say something.

Finally Moira said, "C'mon, let's go to Dungy's."

No one could argue with that. Dungy's Comic and Video Emporium had a weak selection of video games, but there were shelves full of monster models, posters of half-naked girls in soapsuds, and trading cards for movies and TV shows. And then there were the comic books.

Ross could tell you the origin of all the characters in the Marvel Universe or rattle off the name and number of every issue in which Superman died. Whenever he finished with a new Daredevil or Dark Knight, he'd pass it on to me. At first I just liked the pictures, but I'd been getting more and more into the stories. It was only in comic books where a dangerous guy like the Sandman or the Collector could actually be a hero.

Ross flipped through a new issue of *The X-Men* while I checked out the covers. As Moira skipped up behind us, holding out a package of Bubblicious gum, Ross pulled out a wilted dollar bill. "Hey, you got any money I could borrow?" he asked Moira.

"Maybe you shouldn't have bought those DVDs," Moira said.

"I'll pay you back when we get our allowance."

"That's not the point," Moira said, and went into a rant about overspending, even though Ross was right—he'd get fifty dollars on Sunday, so what was the big deal?

Behind us the cashier disappeared below the counter, only his spiked yellow hair showing. Daniel looked at him and then at the cover of *The Collector*, which featured the main character's slash of a face collapsed into a snarl as he studied a woman in a skin-tight dress. And then in one fluid motion Daniel plucked the comic from the rack, crushed it into a tube, and jabbed it in his coat. Fear clogged my throat, but my lips were too numb to form words.

Fortunately, Moira spoke for me. "What the hell?" she hissed, ending her tirade against Ross midword.

Ross hadn't seen Daniel's move. "What the hell what?"

"Nothing," Daniel said, yanking up his jacket's zipper. The comic book was invisible except for a tiny bulge above his heart. Moira whispered into Ross's ear. The cashier glanced over, then away, and Daniel reached for the new *Incredible Hulk*. I nearly passed out.

But this time Daniel brought the comic to the clerk, who punched the cash register with his pinkie. Daniel laid out a ten for him.

As we left the store, Moira asked, "What're you doing?"

Daniel shrugged. "It's nothing."

"It's stealing," Ross said.

"Could you say it any louder? Maybe the goddamn clerk didn't hear you."

"Maybe I should tell him," Moira said.

"You want him to call the cops? On all of us?" Daniel waited for that to sink in. I thought of riding in the back of the sheriff's car, the handcuffs cutting off my circulation, my fingers pawing at a door with no handle. Again I felt some of what I'd felt then—a sick, oozing fear—but also a buzz of energy, like caffeine shot straight into my veins.

I looked at Daniel. "Why'd you buy that other comic when you could've boosted it?"

"If you don't buy anything, it's suspicious."

"The whole thing's suspicious," Moira said. "If you want to be friends with us, you won't ever do *that* again." Although Moira's voice sounded forceful, she looked to me and Ross for support, as if she needed us to make her words true. We both nodded.

"Besides, Travis doesn't need any more trouble right now," Ross said, and I couldn't argue with that.

Moira pulled out her cell phone, barely glancing at it. "We'd better go. We gotta be home by ten."

Her curfew was eleven and I almost said so, but Moira was already off to the exit, Ross a half step behind. Daniel went too, but more slowly. "Hell, if that clerk caught us," he said, "I'd just put him on the list."

"What list?" I asked. Ross and Moira were out of earshot.

"The list of people who need to be shot. I started one in Buffalo—just put down everyone who pissed me off."

"Did it help?"

He shrugged. "Sometimes."

Turning away, I glanced at the nearest row of store windows and saw Koryn inside, posing with a tiger print shirt at her chest. Her friend Laurel laughed as Koryn twirled, still holding the shirt up.

"Why don't you just talk to her?" Daniel asked. "I've seen the way she looks at you in English class."

"I can't just . . . I mean . . ."

Moira looked back suddenly, one hand on her hip. "Are you guys coming or not?" she called.

As I hurried forward, Daniel said, "Sometimes you can't just wait for things to come to you. You've got to go after them. Especially the things you want most."

He's right, you know.

I smiled to myself as I pushed out the door to the parking lot, surprised to find that the night air was warmer than when we'd come in, surprised too to realize that hearing the voice didn't bother me. Either I was getting used to it, or I was starting to like it. Or maybe both.

DANIEL

THIS MUCH WAS CLEAR: Mrs. Saxon had it in for me from the moment I walked into class Monday morning. I'd slept late and didn't get to school until ten minutes into first period. She was already waving her copy of *Wuthering Heights*, Post-Its flapping from the pages like feathers. Although she looked at me with disapproval, she didn't stop her lecture, just kept rambling on about the "arc" of Heathcliff. His name sounded familiar, but all I'd read about so far was a guy named Lockwood and a lot of tea drinking.

When I reached my chair, I found a comic on it, the issue of *The Collector* that Daniel had swiped from Dungy's. As I nodded at him, he mouthed the words, "Keep it."

The Collector was my favorite comic book character. He was a former Mafia hitman who'd been shot so badly he nearly died, but instead of taking him to the afterlife, the Grim Reaper healed him. "Now you can find what's yours," the Reaper had said. "And give people what's theirs." Since then, the Collector had gone around the country delivering what people wanted most. Sometimes it was money, other times a missing child or a long-lost love. But whatever it was, the person who got it usually wished they hadn't. In the opening pages of this issue, a woman was pining for a husband who'd died from cancer. I was curious to find out more but I didn't want to get yelled at, so I hid the book and tried to pay attention.

It wasn't easy. I scanned the room until I found Koryn's halo of brown hair and green braid. I drew her profile, starting in the margins and expanding out to where I should've been taking notes.

At the front of the room, Mrs. Saxon asked something about Heathcliff, and a bunch of hands shot up. Koryn's stayed on her desk, folded neatly. I started to draw her slim fingers.

"I'd like to hear from someone who hasn't participated yet." Mrs. Saxon's words floated into my brain as if from a faraway place. I brought my head down, but she had already zeroed in on me. "Mr. Ellroy, how about you?"

My face started to burn. I knew that everyone was watching me and no matter what I said, it would somehow be wrong. "I, um . . . didn't hear the question," I said.

"Heathcliff. In the introduction, we're told 'he's on an arrow straight course to perdition.' So do you believe he's heading down a dark road, or does he have the ability to veer off, to save himself and Catherine?"

"I think he's . . . he doesn't have any choice. He just, he's doing the only thing he can."

"Mmm, interesting perspective," Mrs. Saxon said, in a way that meant the opposite. "Does anyone disagree? Yes, Jordan."

"I think Heathcliff could've changed his mind at any time," he said. "Just look at how he's so bent on seeing Catherine, even though Lockwood tells him that she's forgotten all about him. If Heathcliff would've just stayed away . . ."

I tuned out the discussion and tried to go back to my drawing, but I couldn't concentrate. When the end of period bell finally buzzed, I jumped up, clapped my notebook shut, and crumpled up the paper I'd drawn on. Daniel looked over and said with a smirk, "See you at lunch, loverboy."

I almost followed him to the door, but I wanted to avoid P.J. and Jordan, and I couldn't get out without going past them. They milled around, so busy talking it took them forever to pick up their stuff.

After P.J. and Jordan finally left, I gave them a count of three before following. I was only halfway to the door when something brushed my shoulder. I jumped.

"I didn't mean to scare you," Koryn said.

My heart thumped loudly. "You didn't."

She glanced over at Mrs. Saxon, who swiped an eraser across the blackboard. "So I guess you don't like *Wuthering Heights,*" she whispered.

"It's slow," I said.

"Well, it actually picks up as you keep going. But still, I'd rather be reading some poetry."

At least poems were short, so I said, "Me too."

Koryn nodded, pleased, and I flung my crumpled sketch at the wastebasket but it bounced off the rim. I reached for it, but Koryn was closer than I was. As she started to drop the paper into the trash, something caught her eye.

"I didn't mean . . . that is, it's not—"

"It's amazing," Koryn said, smoothing out the paper on the wall. "Only it's not done. Would you finish it for me?"

"Sure, but . . . let me start over. I could do better than that."

Koryn's backpack slid off her shoulder, pulling at the edge of her orange shirt to reveal the white line of her bra strap. "Pretty confident, huh?" she said, as I took the sketch back. "All right, I can't wait to see how it turns out."

If not for what happened at lunch, I probably would have dreamed about Koryn all day long. I worked on various sketches of her for most of the next three periods, but I couldn't get them right. The nose was too big or too small, the eyes too close or too far apart. Finally I gave up and went back to the Collector comic, but I couldn't concentrate, and I was rereading the same page for the fourth time when I got on the lunch line.

Amy was ahead of me, and beside her Taffy checked her face in a compact. "Could you believe how hard that pre-calc quiz was?" Taffy asked.

"Oh, it wasn't so bad," Amy said. She saw me looking at her and frowned.

"Hi," I said, turning to Taffy.

"Hi," Taffy said.

And that was it, as far as our conversation would ever go, even as I thought for the millionth time about how good her hug had felt in the vet's office. A sudden sadness washed over me and a kind of courage came with it, and instead of picking up the comic again I said, "Taffy, how's Liz?"

"Liz?" Taffy scrunched her eyebrows together. "Oh, Liz."

Amy looked at me like I had five heads and laughed. "That old dog died like a hundred years ago."

"I've got a German shepherd now," Taffy said. "His name is Eddie. Do you have a dog?"

"No."

That was all I could say, which left me feeling about as big as a turd in a swimming pool. Why hadn't I just left Taffy alone? Rage built up in me as Daniel came over.

"Hey, what's the matter?" he asked.

"Nothing."

"I want to tell you something. But it's a secret."

"Okay," I said without enthusiasm, shoving the comic in my backpack.

"I haven't mentioned this to anybody else, but today's—"

He stopped short as Jordan and P.J. rolled up. Amy kissed Jordan and Taffy pouted until P.J. gave her a kiss that was longer than Jordan and Amy's. P.J. kept his eyes open the whole time and they glinted in his meaty face.

As the line crawled forward, Jordan acted as though he'd just realized they'd cut us in line. "Hey, Travis, you mind?"

"Of course he minds," Daniel said. "And so do I." He pushed away his stringy black hair that hung like old spaghetti. "And what about everybody else? Did you bother to check with them?"

I looked at the rest of the line. Max Monroe picked at the cuff of a faded black T-shirt. Sean Delaney and Tiffany Erstad were staring into space as if wasted, but Tiffany glanced over long enough for me to realize she knew exactly what was going on. If P.J. wanted to muscle in, no one here would stop him.

"Why don't you mind your own business?" P.J. said, his gaze drilling into Daniel.

Jordan tugged at P.J.'s arm. "C'mon, let's just go in back."

"We're not going anywhere," P.J. said, and grabbed a handful of Daniel's shirt. "You got a problem with that?"

If Daniel had shaken his head no, just like I would have, maybe everything would've been fine. But Daniel said, "I've got no problem except . . . do you really *need* lunch? I mean, I read somewhere that whales eat their own fat. Is that true?"

I started to smile until P.J. thumped Daniel against the tile wall. My lips straightened as Daniel's fingers clenched into fists. He's not going to back down, I thought, and felt a new kind of fear.

You going to let your buddy do this alone, Trav-oh? Get in there. Get in there and fight.

But I didn't want to fight. I started to back away, only instead of charging Daniel, P.J. lunged at me. He clamped his fingers around my wrist and twisted, bringing my arm up hard behind me. I bit my lip and forced myself to hold the tears in the corners of my eyes. P.J. tightened his grip, yanking my arm so hard the muscles felt stretched to their breaking point.

"Come on, Peej, leave him alone," Jordan said, but P.J. only twisted harder.

"P.J., don't hurt him," Taffy said. "Please."

Amy said nothing.

Do something, you wuss.

Tasting my own tears and choking on terror, I lashed out with my foot, aiming for P.J.'s groin but catching him in the thigh. P.J. grunted and lost his balance just long enough for me to pull away. He groped toward me, cursing, as Jordan hissed: "Watch out."

At first I thought he was talking to me. But when I opened my eyes Beth Kittinger stood there, smoothing out the front of her checkered skirt. "What's going on here, boys?"

"Travis and I were just goofing around," P.J. said.

Jordan put a hand on my elbow, as if he cared. "You all right, Travis?"

I snapped my arm away, the muscles throbbing. "I'm fine."

"Are you sure, Travis?" Beth asked.

"Sure I'm sure," I said, noticing that Daniel was looking at her legs. The checkered skirt didn't quite cover her knees.

"I don't want you getting into any more trouble, P.J."

"But I wasn't—"

"*Do you* understand *me?*" She looked from Daniel to me and then back to P.J.

P.J. nodded. Beth looked at me again, her forehead crinkling in concern. Then she nodded and left.

As he started for the kitchen doorway, P.J. said, "Guess you'd better thank that bitch for saving your bacon, Travis. And your new boss too."

It took a second for that to sink in. My new boss?

"Jesus, P.J.," Jordan said. "You're not supposed to say . . ." He looked at me and added, "Gus was going to announce it at work today."

Blood pounded inside my head and it felt like my insides had been shredded with claws. All I could think about was how I'd been at Coffee Time longer than Jordan and had started doing everything Gus asked me to, but it didn't matter, he still got the promotion.

As I turned away, P.J. grabbed my arm, and anger surged through me. My hand curled into a fist, but he wasn't fazed.

"One more thing, Travis. I'm tired of waiting for my money."

The mix of anger, disappointment, and fear left me flustered. The fist loosened. "No, listen . . . I, um, I'm just—"

"I want the first half in a week. That's a hundred and fifty next Monday."

"Dream on," Daniel said.

"Oh yeah?" P.J. was grinning now. "Let's make it Friday then. Unless you want to move it up even further?"

I shook my head no and hurried away. Face burning, hands shaking, I steamrolled past the library to the side exit. I blinked against the sudden assault of daylight, my nostrils full of the smell of burnt leaves. Walking quickly, I heard the sound of footsteps behind me. It was Daniel.

"I'm sorry," Daniel said. "About P.J. I didn't mean to make the trouble with him any worse than it is."

Friday. I knew that I'd never have enough money by then. Crunching numbers anyway, I started walking. Daniel caught up to me quickly.

"Seems like Ross and Moira are loaded," he said. "Can't you borrow some money from them?"

"It's my problem, not theirs."

"Have you even asked?"

"No," I said, although I'd thought about it.

"But they must've offered to help."

"No. It's my problem and—"

"Bullshit. They're your friends and they've got a ton of money, they ought to lend you a little. Hell, they're so rich, they ought to *give* you the cash."

"It's no big deal," I said.

"Okay, fine. Anyway, I'm sorry about that promotion thing. That sucks. Of course you know why Jordan got it, don't you? He's a total kiss ass. You saw him in class today. He just sucks up to everyone."

"I don't care, all right. I'm going home."

"Wait." Daniel shifted his eyes to the ground, studying his sneakers. "You know that thing I was going to tell you . . . ah, forget it."

"Well, what is it already?"

He looked up suddenly. "Today's my birthday. And I don't really know anybody or anything, so I just thought maybe you could come to my house for a while and . . . never mind."

He started to walk away. But before he turned I saw his loneliness clinging like a film. So I said, "Maybe I could come over for a bit. But I've got to work this afternoon."

"What time?" he asked, suddenly cheerful.

"Three-thirty."

"That still gives us a couple of hours."

Turning to the road, I froze. A shiny white Shadwell Police car cruised past. The sun blasted off its side window and I couldn't tell who was at the wheel. But I watched and waited and said, "Okay, let's go."

New York State Police
interview with Madeline Pulver

DET. UPSHAW: How well did you know Travis?

MADELINE: I only saw him a couple of times, maybe two or three.

DET. UPSHAW: I understand that he was your son's best friend.

MADELINE: Oh no. They were friendly, but that's all.

DET. UPSHAW: Did Daniel ever talk about Travis with you?

MADELINE: Not really. At first he did say Travis was nice. Later, he started to wonder if Travis was a little . . . unbalanced.

DET. UPSHAW: Was that the word Daniel used?

MADELINE: I can't remember. That was what he meant, that Travis was unbalanced, off somehow.

DET. UPSHAW: And what did you personally think of Travis?

MADELINE: He was quiet, polite, unassuming. I thought maybe he'd be a good influence on Daniel. Not that . . . never mind.

DET. UPSHAW: Mrs. Pulver, your former neighbor here in Shadwell, Mrs. Barker, had some things to say about Daniel.

MADELINE: That woman is insane.

DET. UPSHAW: Perhaps. But I've also spoken to a couple of detectives in Buffalo. They said Daniel had been accused of shoplifting. Do you know anything about that?

MADELINE: The accusations, of course. But that's all
   they were.

DET. UPSHAW: What about this young man, Paul Feezer, who—

MADELINE: That's it. I want my lawyer.

DET. UPSHAW: Mrs. Pulver, please, just—stop the tape, all
   right? There's no reason to—

"I TOLD MY FOLKS I wasn't going to move again," Daniel said, pacing around the wooden island in his spotless kitchen. "Two goddamn years left in high school, you'd think maybe, just maybe, we could stay put. But no. So I'll finish up school in a couple years and that's it, I'm gone." He paused. "You want a . . . soda or something?" He was careful not to call it "pop."

"Sure," I said.

He found a couple of root beers and a yellow apple in the fridge, then pulled out a pocketknife with a flat, thin blade. My brother had had a knife just like it when he was in the Boy Scouts.

As Daniel worked the blade through the apple's skin, my stomach growled with hunger. On the stool beside me was a wad of mail Daniel had brought in. One envelope was bright purple with Daniel's name in flowery writing and a Buffalo postmark.

"How many places have you lived?" I asked.

"Let's see, Chicago, Detroit, Buffalo—and that's just since I was eleven." Daniel slashed at the thick pieces of apple, cutting until there were two dozen chunks. "It's a job thing. Not my mom's job, she's a computer programmer. But my dad's a CEO, kind of. He just gets hired to come in and fire people and make the stock look good. Then he takes off."

"Wow, a CEO," I said, wondering if Daniel's father had an office with a view and a secretary, which my father had always wanted. "He must be smart."

"Yeah, well, if he was so smart maybe he'd be able to find a way that I wouldn't have to change schools every time I take a shit."

Daniel speared a piece of apple on the knife tip and held it out.

As I reached for it, he jabbed the knife at me and I jumped. He pulled off the piece of apple and set it in front of me. Despite my hunger, I pushed it away. Daniel folded up the knife, then grabbed the purple envelope and jumped up, leaving the mail and the rest of the apple on the counter.

"Come on," he said. "I want to show you something."

I followed Daniel upstairs. The house smelled of fresh paint, the walls as smooth as vanilla frosting. Daniel led me past the first open door to a bedroom twice as big as mine. It had an old-style captain's bed and a matching cabinet and computer desk. A pile of moving boxes made a tower in the corner and the walls were blank.

Daniel dropped the purple envelope on the desk and grabbed a blank yellow pad. On the top sheet, he wrote in his cramped but neat scrawl: LIST OF PEOPLE WHO NEED TO BE SHOT. Under that he added #1—P.J. RILEY.

"Who should be next?" Daniel asked.

I hesitated. "Gus, my boss, for giving Jordan that raise."

Instead of writing, Daniel handed the pen to me. I hesitated and then I wrote GUS BENEDICT. I liked the feeling of making these lines, watching the lines take on the shape of letters, the letters forming a name.

"What about Mrs. Saxon?" Daniel asked. "She humiliated you, made you look like a complete jackass."

"I'll let her slide," I said, surprised by the power of those words. "This time."

"All right."

"But what do we do with it?" I asked, studying the page.

"You take it," he said. "For now."

Folding up the list, I noticed a photo on Daniel's desk, sticking out beneath a pile of loose papers. It showed Daniel and a boy with thick glasses standing side by side in the woods, both with huge smiles.

"This is for you," Daniel said.

"Huh?" When I looked up, he held out a blank sketch pad. I took it from him, flipping through the clean white pages, touching the spiral binding at the top.

"It's so you don't have to keep drawing on notebook paper," he said. "And you can have all your sketches in one place."

I touched the cardboard cover, amazed. I couldn't remember the last time anyone had gotten me a gift besides my parents. And even though this didn't cost very much, that didn't matter. I felt as good as if he'd given me a new car.

"Come on," Daniel said, moving to the doorway.

I stuck the list in my pocket and followed him back down the hall to the master bedroom. He circled the bed, crouching at a nightstand with silver legs, and slid out a drawer full of rolled-up socks. Slipping his hand in, he unearthed a couple of *Playboy*s. I was looking at one of the covers—*College Coeds Reveal All*—when Daniel leaned forward and pulled out a gun.

He pointed it at my chest, less than four feet from me. I stared into the two pencil-tip sized holes at the end of the weapon. "Bang," he said, as I took a sudden step back, nearly tripping over a high-heeled shoe. Daniel laughed. "Relax. It's not even loaded."

He held it out to me, its matte-black finish catching the sunlight.

"Take it."

My legs felt like jelly as I gazed at the sleek black barrel. The only gun I had ever seen up close was Richie's .22 Remington. My father had bought it for Richie's twelfth birthday and they'd taken it out to the backyard to fire at an old tire. "Just keep your hands steady," my father said, "and look right down the sight." Richie hit the tire again and again, the soft pops of the .22 sounding like an old man's cough. I kept pestering them for a turn but my father said I was too young.

After the first couple of weeks, Richie seemed to forget about the new rifle but I never did. It was in his closet, on a top shelf where I couldn't reach, and whenever I played with my toy guns—hand-me-downs from Richie—I fantasized about the real thing. Richie only took the rifle out three or four times a year after that, and I always went with him. He never hunted animals, just fired at the same old tires from the shed.

"Come on," Daniel said, still holding out the gun. "Take it already."

To my surprise, I did. I closed my hand around the checkered grip, which was cool against my skin, and curled my finger inside the trigger guard. The sore muscles in my arm tightened as I lifted it, and I winced. Remembering what my father once told Richie—never aim at anyone, even if the gun's not loaded—I pointed out the window, where a group of birds perched on a tree branch.

"Have you ever shot it?" I asked.

"Lots of times. My dad's favorite saying is 'Guns aren't dangerous, ignorance is dangerous,' so yeah, he totally wants me to know how to use it." Daniel laughed and reached for the gun. "Come on. Let's take it out for a test-drive."

"I don't know if that's such a good idea."

"Why not?"

"I'm going to have to go soon," I said. "To work."

"Screw work. Look at how they treat you there, giving your promotion to Jordan."

"But I need the money to—"

"Look, do you want to do this or not?"

I thought about the pay I'd lose and the money I owed P.J., not to mention the lecture Gus would give me about shirking my responsibilities. Despite all that the answer was yes, I did want to do this.

"I've got to at least call in."

"Don't worry about it," Daniel said, the gun dangling at his side. It sounded more like a command than a suggestion. He led the way downstairs, and I left my new sketch pad by the front door, half wishing I could just go off and draw in it.

Our coats were still at school, but Daniel found two extras in the closet. They were identical, except that one was blue and the other green. Yanking up the hood on the green one, I jogged after Daniel, who had the gun in his pocket and a plastic bag of soda cans at his side. The sky had turned the color of dirty mop water. As the trees thinned out, the wind bit at my cheeks and sucked the heat from my fingers and toes. Fall had arrived, and I could already taste winter beneath it.

"Do you ever miss Buffalo?" I asked.

"What's to miss?" Daniel said.

I thought about the purple envelope that had come in the mail, and the picture of him with the boy in the thick glasses. "I don't know, old friends."

"I knew some people, but they weren't my friends." Then he smiled. "Oh, you mean the letter? That's from Caitlin, an old girlfriend, sort of. It was more of a sex thing."

"But she writes to you."

"And e-mails. IMs too. Shit, if I could be with her, that would be one thing . . . but I don't need a bunch of gooey love letters."

"Maybe she just wanted to wish you a happy birthday."

He stepped over a bunch of dead branches. "What about you?"

"What about me?"

"No girlfriend, I guess. You're probably still a virgin."

I wanted to deny it but didn't.

"So how far've you gone?" he asked. "Second base? First?"

"Second," I lied. "Once."

"With who?"

I hesitated. The first name that came to mind was Koryn, but I said the next: "Moira." Even as I wondered if that would be enough to satisfy him, I heard myself blurting, "It was last year. We were both really drunk. You know how it is." I hoped like hell that he did know, since I didn't. "But don't say anything about it, Moira'll get pissed."

"Sweet," Daniel said, nodding. I didn't know which he liked better, me getting some action from Moira or that it was supposed to be a secret.

The truth was Moira and I *had* kissed, once. Ross was away at a computer seminar and we were alone, watching a movie on their big screen TV, when she leaned over and pressed her lips to mine.

"What the hell was that?" I asked.

She lay back on the couch. "I just wanted to see what you'd do."

"I'm not doing anything," I said, and she laughed. I felt my face going red, even as excitement stirred in me, but whatever had prompted Moira to kiss me was gone. She made me swear not to tell anyone, even Ross, and until that afternoon, I'd kept my promise.

Daniel stopped at a spot where fallen branches and a rock outcropping formed a natural wall and said, "Perfect." In the distance, I heard the muffled pops of rifle shots and crows cawing overhead, flapping toward safety.

Daniel dropped the bag of cans, then brought the gun out of his pocket. At first I felt the same fear I'd had in his parents' bedroom, but it quickly faded. Daniel popped the magazine out of the handle. "I need some slugs," he said. "They're in my pocket."

I found the cardboard box and plucked some of the bullets out. They were gold hollow points with silver in the middle of their backs, the tips scooped out like ice cream cones someone had stuck their tongue into. Daniel lined the slugs up one next to the other inside the magazine.

"They're called hollow points," he said, taking the last of them from my palm.

"I know," I said, but I didn't tell him it was only from the movies.

He slammed the magazine back into the gun with the heel of his hand, then held out the weapon.

"I don't know what to do with it," I said.

"Just hold it."

The gun seemed heavier than it had in the bedroom. Either it was the weight of the bullets or just my imagination.

He set up four cans on the edge of the log, then stepped back about twenty feet and drew a line in the dirt with his sneaker.

"I'll go first," he said, taking the gun. "Seeing as how I'm the birthday boy."

He closed his fingers around the grip, aiming the barrel straight out. As he squinted down the back of the gun, I thought maybe he was going to change his mind about firing it, but then his finger snapped back. There was a sound like a train roaring down the tracks and a tongue of yellow flame.

On the log, the cans stood unmoved.

"Shit. Well, you give it a try." Daniel held out the gun, pointing at a tiny switch on the lower right side above the grip. "And don't turn the safety off until you're ready."

I studied every detail of the weapon: the three-arrowed logo on the handle, the words PIETRO BERETTA on the nose, the tiny sight that rose from its tip like a pimple.

"You're holding it wrong," Daniel said, readjusting the gun so that it was flush against my palm. "And you're not standing right either." He adjusted my hips so that my legs weren't spread so far apart, then said, "All you do is look down the sight and get this little bump on the tip of the gun to line up between these bumps in back."

I stared down the barrel, trying to arrange the three little nubs one in front of the other, but they kept jumping around. My forearm was sore from the weight of the gun and the blood throbbed in my ears. I tried to focus on a root beer can but it seemed a million miles away.

You can do it, Trav-oh. Come on, come on.

The trigger was like an icicle against my finger. I don't need to do this, I told myself, but I glanced over at Daniel and knew that I did. I thought again of going out in the woods with Richie and my father, wishing I was the one with the rifle.

Wham bam, just go. Just do it.

Fine, I thought, just once, and brought my finger against the trigger ever so slightly, and then a little more. BOOM! It was as though two lions stood on either side of me and roared as one while a kung fu expert jump kicked my arms. Adrenaline swirled in my veins and the ringing in my ears went on and on.

Daniel said something, but I couldn't hear it at first.

"What?" I shouted.

"I said, you looked like a natural."

He pointed at a hole in a branch about six inches above the cans. It was no bigger than the width of a Slurpee straw. "Aim a little lower next time," he said.

I squinted down the barrel, lining up the log in the sights and aiming an inch below one of the root beers. I fired. The can leaped backward with a high-pitched plink, tumbling end over end into the branches.

My scalp was tingling and I suddenly felt ten feet tall. This, I knew, was what it was like to make an eighty-yard touchdown with your team behind by six. This was what it felt like to be a champion.

Daniel and I each had a few more turns, though it took him four tries to nail his first can. I was too jittery to hit any more targets, but I was looking forward to shooting again when he said, "It's getting dark. Late too."

Daniel and I gathered the cans, then rooted around for the spent shells. He gave me the fallen root beer can, which had a charred black hole in its side. I held it with a sense of wonder.

"My mother should be home by now," he said, slipping the gun in his pocket. "And she might be pissed that you're here. I'm not supposed to have anyone over."

"But it's your birthday."

"It doesn't matter. Trust me."

When we got back to the house, a woman who was as tall as my father and looked ten years younger than my mother stood in the middle of the kitchen. Her feathered blond hair drifted over a tired face and her nose, mouth, and eyes tightened into a smile when she saw Daniel. "Hey, you should've left a note." I noticed that she had cleaned up the pieces of apple from the counter.

"We were out," Daniel said, opening the flap on his right pocket, the one where he had stashed the gun.

"Of course you were out, but I didn't know where." She pushed at her hair as if to comb it in place, but it was already perfectly set. "Take your jacket off, Dan, and stay awhile."

Daniel didn't respond to being called "Dan," just pulled his zipper down.

His mother turned to me. "I'm Madeline Pulver."

"Travis," I said as she put her hand out. Her fingers were thin but her grip was strong.

"Do you go to school with Danny?" she asked. Danny?

"We're in English together," I said.

Daniel put his hand in his pocket, the one with the gun in it, and I felt a lurch in my stomach. "Mom, can Travis stay for dinner?"

His mother turned to the counter and tore the wrapper off a wine bottle. "I only picked up enough food for the three of us, if your father ever gets home. Another time."

"But it's my—"

The word "birthday" lingered on his lips, but she cut him off. "Another time, okay, Danny?" There was a sliver of unease in her voice. She jabbed a corkscrew at the bottle but it wouldn't go in. "Besides, I think I'm getting a headache."

Daniel's hand rose from his pocket. He grabbed the corkscrew from his mother and twisted it into the bottle. "Thank you," she said quietly as he pulled it out. But he turned away to the front door without responding.

"Good night, Mrs. Pulver," I said, shedding the coat Daniel had lent me. I left it on a chair by the door and picked up my new sketch pad. Daniel's mother didn't say a word as he led me out.

Full darkness had nearly touched down. Up the road, a woman with a tangle of gray hair over a long coat wrestled with a tall black dog on a leash. "Alfie!" she called, but he kept barking and pulling her into the bushes.

"Damn dog," Daniel said.

"I can't believe it," I said as Daniel's mother's shadow drifted across the living-room window. "She didn't even say happy birthday."

"She doesn't care. All she wants to do is to get trashed."

I thought of my father, who was probably on his second or third beer by now, and reached into my pocket, feeling the rough edge where the bullet had pierced the can. Daniel and I slapped fists, one on top of the other, and as he turned to go he said, "If your new boss gives you a hard time about missing work, you know what to do."

I touched my front pocket. "Put him on the list."

"See, you learn quick."

I clutched my sketch pad to my chest and fingered the hole in the can as I half walked, half ran home. The woman with the dog had disappeared inside her house, its windows concealed by yellowing curtains. As I moved to avoid a pile of dog shit, my pinkie caught on one of the ragged edges of aluminum. I sucked blood off my finger, wondering when Daniel would take me out shooting again.

First day in charge at work. Gus wasn't there. Emergency root canal. Travis bailed, too. That left me and Koryn.

Gus called just after four. From the dentist's office. He could barely talk. Said something like, "Wow's wings wat wuh wore?"

"Fine," I said, and then he asked about Travis. I told him he'd called in sick. Okay, he hadn't. But Gus would've been pissed, and I felt sort of responsible for Travis not being there because of that mess with P.J. at lunch.

Around four-thirty I told Koryn she could have some coffee or something, even though you're not supposed to drink on the job. I said I'd make her a cappuccino, but she didn't want one. She started pouring vanilla syrup into a plastic cup. Then she added skim milk. Weird.

When we were having our drinks, she said, "So I think our first stop should be Williamsburg." I must've looked clueless, so she added, "In Virginia, you know."

Then I remembered what we'd talked about last time. Taking a trip. Being explorers.

"Why Williamsburg?" I asked, smiling.

"You know, they have those people dressed up like in Colonial times, and they talk like they're really from back then. It might be cheesy, but I think it'd be fun. Besides, I was looking at some pictures online and the area's really pretty. Especially in the fall."

"Okay."

"But you know what this means."

"What's that?"

"You've got to pick the next stop," she said.

I started to say something but she shook her head.

"Uh-uh, not yet. Think about it."

Places ran through my head. I could see the map. Virginia cutting out into the Atlantic. So many choices from there. South. Or west. And how far to go?

After we closed I picked up Amy and we went to Taffy's. Her parents were at some kind of charity dinner, wouldn't be home until late. Me, P.J., Taffy, and Amy smoked some endo and watched *Platoon*. P.J. loves his war movies. He sat a couple feet in front of the TV so he could see well enough. He knows it by heart, anyway.

Halfway through the flick, P.J. and Taffy went upstairs. Amy and I took the sofa. We had fun. Then Amy stood, wrapped in a blanket. Asked me: "What're you thinking about?"

I hate it when she says that. What am I supposed to tell her? "I was just thinking that you're really pretty" or something, I guess. And of course she is. But that's not what I was thinking.

So I said, "I don't know."

"Of course you know. It's your brain."

From upstairs I heard P.J. and Taffy. "Come on," Amy said. "Tell me."

Amy's fingers were on my thigh. Down to the knee, touching my scar. Taffy cried out.

"I was just thinking that I love you," I said.

I don't know where that came from. Maybe I do love Amy. I've been wondering, anyway. But I wasn't planning to say it. Not yet.

Too late.

She threw her arms around me. The blanket was rough and itchy. I pulled Amy closer. Her hair tickled. "I love you, too," she said. Over and over. Like the first day of school, when she said how much she missed me.

After that Amy didn't ask what I was thinking about again. Or who. I was glad. I didn't want to lie. Not after we said we loved each other.

"WHAT HAPPENED TO YOU GUYS yesterday?" Moira asked as Daniel and I carried our trays to the table.

"Nothing," I said, sliding onto the bench across from her. She had laid out her lunch with surgical precision, a hard-boiled egg here and a bag of potato chips there, while Ross had torn through his paper sack to get what he wanted. Lunch wasn't his main focus anyway. He clutched a video game the size of a wallet with a full-color screen and 3-D graphics.

Over his shoulder, I saw a muscular soldier unleash a rattle of machine gun fire on a horde of aliens. When the creatures got hit their bodies trembled and green blood oozed out. The images were so sharp and real I couldn't believe it.

"Is that the new GameBox?" Daniel asked.

"Just got it last night," Ross said. "It's really sweet."

Most kids just played video games on their phones or on their computers, but Ross always had to get the latest, best system around. Every kid wanted the GameBox but almost no one could afford it. I'd never seen it go for any less than $350 online.

I pulled out my new sketch pad, picking at my food with one hand, drawing with the other.

"So what happened with you and P.J. yesterday?" Moira asked.

Before I could speak, Daniel jumped into the story of the lunch line incident, and I didn't point out where his version split off from reality. He ended with—"and then I told him, if he messes with us again, I'll cut his balls off"—keeping his voice low enough so that no one could overhear him. That was for the best, because P.J. sat two tables over, attacking a pile of sloppy joe with his spork.

"You better be careful with P.J.," Moira said. "He may be an asshole, but he's a dangerous asshole."

"He's such an asshole, we ought to put him on the list twice," I said, adding a new touch to the picture I'd been drawing. It showed an alien like the one in Ross's video game, with a half-eaten P.J. hanging out of its mouth.

"What list?" Ross asked, without looking up, and then I realized my mistake. Moira's eyes held me.

" 'Put him on the list,' " I said, closing up my sketch pad. "You know, it's just a saying."

I looked at Daniel for help, which only made Moira more curious. " 'You reap what you sow' is a saying, and so is 'an eye for an eye,' " she said. "But I never heard any saying about a list."

"Well, do you know every saying in the world?" I asked.

"Of course not, but I know most of them."

"Oh yeah?" Daniel said. "You ever heard someone say 'it's like standing on a pissdyke'?"

"Standing on a what?"

"You heard me."

Daniel shook his head at her. Moira's stare challenged me to speak up but I didn't. Her eyes narrowed as she said, "Of course I've heard of standing on a pissdyke," and I wanted to jump in and say that Daniel was kidding. But it was too late.

Daniel smiled. "Then what does it mean?"

"I don't have to tell you."

"You can't," he said, his lips scaling back from his teeth. "I just made it up."

Ross laughed as Moira picked at the remains of her peanut butter sandwich. I turned away and saw Koryn framed by the cafeteria doorway. Her loose drawstring pants clung to her legs as she glided to the stairs, green braid swishing in her dark hair.

Oh yeah, she's a hottie. Hottest thing in this hellhole.

Daniel laughed, as if he knew what the voice had said. "Man, you cream your pants every time she goes by."

"I do not," I said, thinking that someday I'd go up and tug on her braid, and she'd turn to me. I'd move my fingers roughly across her skin, sliding them down the curving line of her back and reaching inside the waistband of her pants until—

"Don't be such a pig, Daniel," Moira said. "Besides, Koryn's out of Travis's league."

Daniel frowned. "That's a pretty foul thing to say."

"You want next, Travis?" Ross asked.

"Sure," I said, following Ross's lead in ignoring them. I pressed the start button on the GameBox. My alter ego appeared, alternately firing his machine gun and leaping into the air as I got a feel for the controls.

Meanwhile, Moira locked eyes with Daniel. "All I'm saying is that Travis and Koryn are in different leagues, and people should stay where they belong. That's the way it is."

"Oh, I know how it is," Daniel said, a wink in his voice. I pushed the fire button frantically, sure that Daniel was going to spill the beans on my bullshit makeout session with Moira. On the screen, creatures lunged at my alter ego so quickly I couldn't keep up with them.

"You got a lot of games for that?" Daniel asked.

"I only downloaded a couple so far," Ross said.

Moira didn't add anything, and I was surprised. She never missed a chance to brag. And then I heard: "Hey, when do I get *my* turn?"

P.J.'s voice was unmistakable.

"It's not mine," I said, trying to focus on the aliens instead of him.

"I guess you can't afford one. Too busy saving up for my new window."

Daniel leaned back from the table. "Piss off, P.J."

" 'Piss off, P.J.' " His imitation made Daniel sound high-pitched and pathetic. "Remember, Travis, Friday's payday. Friday. Friiiiii-*day.*"

I swallowed the lump in my throat, the game forgotten in my hands. "I remember but listen, P.J., I might not have all of it."

"Oh, you'll have it. Or else."

Or else what? Come on, don't take his shit, Trav-oh.

From the other table Taffy waved, and P.J.'s attention shifted to her. As he started over, funeral music began to dribble out of the GameBox, and I felt my whole body tense.

"You lost," Moira said.

"So what?" I asked, slamming the game against the table.

Ross winced. "Careful."

"Sorry," I said, but I wasn't, and as I watched P.J. settle in beside Taffy, I realized something: he was glad I didn't have the money. He wanted an excuse to hurt me, and this was as good as any. I looked up at Daniel and he nodded, as if he'd known all along and was waiting for me to catch up.

"How much does one of those go for?" Daniel asked, gesturing at the GameBox.

"I don't know," Ross said. "My dad bought it."

I almost chimed in with the number, but decided not to.

"What's it matter?" Moira asked suspiciously.

"It doesn't. Except that whatever you guys spent on that you could've given to Travis. Helped him keep P.J. off his back."

I looked down at the table, embarrassed. But I wanted to hear what my friends had to say for themselves.

"My dad bought it for me," Ross said. "I'm broke again."

"So am I," Moira said.

But I knew she wasn't. She kept a stash of bills hidden inside the belly of an old teddy bear. Last I'd seen she had more than five hundred dollars in there.

"Besides, I know better than to get involved with P.J.," Moira said.

"P.J. ought to know better than to get involved with me," Daniel said. "Jock or no jock, he's no better than we are. I'm not scared of him, and you don't need to be either, Travis."

I started to laugh then, the kind of laughter that comes out of your mouth and your nose at the same time, that fills your throat until you can barely breathe. The laughter was so strong I couldn't stop it, even though Moira stared at me as if there was something wrong. She squeezed her hands together and glanced at Daniel, as if she wished he would disappear.

After a minute or so the laughter dissolved into a hacking cough and I pressed a napkin to my mouth. "Sorry," I said, realizing that to my friends I must have looked normal again. But in my head, the laughter kept going.

Although I was supposed to go to Ross and Moira's after school, I didn't. I told them I had a lot of homework. Ross shrugged it off, but Moira looked at me like she was going to ask a question and yet wasn't sure she wanted to know the answer. "Tomorrow then," she said on her way to the bus.

As Daniel and I left school, I had assumed we would go to his house, but he said his mother was at home.

"Well, okay," I said. "Why don't we go to the mall then?"

"We've *been* to the mall. Let's go to your place."

"It's not such a good idea."

"Why not?"

My house was the last place I wanted to bring Daniel, so I told him that I didn't have any cool video games and we'd just be bored. "I don't care about that," he said. "Unless you can come up with one good reason, I want to go to your place."

There was a good reason, but not one that I could share. He and his parents lived in a bright new house with airy rooms and skylights. My house was old and dusty with dark cramped rooms so thick with dust and memories of Richie you could barely breathe. When Daniel saw it, he would know how awful my life really was.

I dreaded every second of the walk home. When I finally led him to my bedroom, I stood with my hands in my pockets and a knot in my stomach as he looked around the tiny gray space.

Daniel studied the room, touching the edges of *The Matrix* and *South Park* posters over my desk and the Eminem poster behind the door, all of them held in place with black pushpins. He rifled through the CDs stacked next to my boom box and ran his finger along the spines of the graphic novels on a shelf over my bed. I said suddenly, "I should've had the other room, the bigger one. After my brother Richie went to college, I was supposed to move in there. But he came back after only a few months. And then . . . I got stuck in here."

"How about after he killed himself?" Daniel asked. "Why couldn't you move in then?"

I'd never told Daniel that Richie had killed himself and I was pretty sure Ross and Moira hadn't said anything either. Wondering how much else he knew, I shrugged. "At first, my parents thought it would be disrespectful. Later . . . well, they never gave me a reason, they just said it wouldn't be right."

"Right for who? You? Or them?" He shook his head slowly, then his eyes found me. "You were supposed to have the room, they promised you. They *owed* it to you. That's wrong, Travis. But that's how parents are. They're selfish, they're mean, they're petty. They hate us, and they'll do anything they can to punish us. You know why? They're jealous. They go to work, they come home, they never do the things they did when they were kids. They hate their lives, and

75

I don't blame them. But do they have to take it out on us? God, I'd love to teach them a lesson sometime. Wouldn't you?"

"It's fine," I said quietly. "I don't care about the room anymore." But Daniel was talking about more than the room, I understood that. I reached for the root beer can with the bullet hole that I'd set beside my desk lamp.

"Screw your parents," Daniel said. "If you want to move in there, you should do it. Just do it."

"Look, I can't."

"Yes, you can." Daniel's gaze was unrelenting.

"I've got bigger problems right now, anyway."

"Like what? P.J.?"

"Well, yeah. I haven't got his money. I'm not even close."

"How much do you need?"

"I've got seventy bucks, and I don't get paid again until Saturday. Of course that'll only be another thirty. So I still need fifty, plus a hundred and fifty more for next time."

"We'll get the money somehow."

"How? By robbing a bank?"

Daniel shook his head. "We'll get it," he said, as if he was repeating some kind of self-help mantra. I didn't quite believe him, but I felt better, because he'd said "we" instead of just "you."

Daniel and I headed to the kitchen to get a couple of sodas, but when I turned he wasn't there. Then I heard a scratching sound, and I found him outside Richie's old room. He was jabbing the blade of his pocketknife into the keyhole, working it hard.

"What're you doing?" I asked.

Instead of answering, he jiggled the knife around some more.

"Daniel, what the hell are you doing?"

"How long has this room been locked?"

"A long time. Now stay out of there."

That's right, you tell him. He can't push you around. No-body can.

But he kept moving the knife around, his brows pulled together in concentration, and I was afraid that one more poke or twist would make the knob turn smoothly in his hand.

"I'm serious, Daniel."

"So am I." He looked at me, his hand still working at the lock. "This was supposed to be yours, anyway, right? So it's not even tres-passing."

"Yes, it is," I said, so loudly I surprised myself. I moved forward, my hands coming up. I shoved Daniel in the chest and he stumbled back, losing his grip on the knife.

There you go, Trav-oh. Now we're talking.

The knife hung in the knob before gravity caught up to it and the blade crashed into the hardwood. Kneeling to get it, I noticed a small white nick in the floor.

"Sorry," I muttered, folding up the thin blade.

Daniel took the knife from me, looking surprised but not dis-pleased. "So you *can* stand up for yourself. Or maybe it's just Richie you stand up for."

"Leave me alone," I said, but the words lacked the force and spontaneity of the shove.

"What're you afraid of, Travis? What the hell's in there?"

I shrugged as if I didn't care, but the truth was I didn't know. I hadn't been in there for six years, not since the month after Richie's funeral.

"I've got to get home," Daniel said. "My mom'll be expect-ing me."

I probably should've argued for him to stay. I didn't.

When he left I locked myself in my room, still shaken, and fin-ished reading the new issue of *The Collector*.

The Collector, after finding this woman who mourned her dead husband, had made a deal with her. If he gave her what she wanted most, she'd have to give *him* something, only he wouldn't tell her what. She agreed, insisting that her husband had to look just like he had before the cancer, before chemotherapy. The Collector said they had a deal, and told the woman to wait three nights.

On the third night, there was a citywide blackout, and she waited by the window, in candlelight. Then she heard a knock and jumped up to answer the door. Her husband was there and she hugged him, kissed him, and he was exactly the same as she remembered.

Only he couldn't talk, or wouldn't. No matter what she tried, he just stared blankly at her like a living doll. Finally, the Collector appeared behind the woman, as if he'd appeared out of thin air.

"What's wrong with him?" she asked.

"Nothing's wrong with him. Only he can't talk or think. He's basically a living doll. But he looks just like he did before he got sick. As you requested," the Collector said, and laughed and laughed.

"Take him back."

"I'm afraid I can't do that. Besides, we have a deal. I give you something and you give me something."

"So what do you want?" she asked, sobbing.

"Your life," he said, and handed a straight razor to the dead man. The woman whirled away and tried to run but her husband grabbed her arm and slashed at her elbow. He lost his grip on her for a moment and she tried to get away, but he caught up to her near the window, pinning her against the wall. In one swift stroke, he slashed his wife's throat and lapped up the blood like a cat with a bowl of milk. The last panel showed the Collector, a shadow among shadows, heading for the door as the candle flickered out behind him.

New York State Police
interview with Beth Kittinger

DET. UPSHAW: Tell me how Travis had changed by the time
  you saw him again in high school.
BETH: It's hard to say . . . he'd always been sensitive, shy
  too, but he'd become a little more outgoing. Of course he
  didn't have much self-confidence, not like Richie. And
  Travis was so . . . I guess the only word for it is sad. But
  it was like he didn't know how to release his sadness, and
  I guess that's what made his anger so dangerous.
DET. UPSHAW: But you tried to help him deal with those
  emotions, didn't you? The anger, the sadness. . . .
BETH: Yes, of course. I did everything I could.
DET. UPSHAW: I'm just trying to understand the situation,
  the relationship you had with him.
BETH: Our relationship was the same as I had with all
  the students.
DET. UPSHAW: But he was more than a student. You'd once
  dated his older brother. You knew him, you knew his
  family. You even talked to his mother about him.
BETH: Well, yes, she called me up, the first week of school,
  and we met at her bank for an hour or two. She was
  concerned. She asked me if I could watch him, make sure
  he was okay. She called every couple of days for an
  update. I kept telling her he was fine. I thought he was. I
  figured he was dealing with normal stuff, girls and
  bullies and overprotective parents. (WHISPERS) I thought I
  was getting through to him . . . I thought everything
  would be all right.

"I'VE GOT TO GO IN the back and check on the orders," Jordan said, looking around Coffee Time as if he owned the place. "You know what to do out here."

"Sure," I said, rubbing my hands on my stained green apron. Jordan's apron was crisp and neat, creases pressed into the brown cotton. "Whatever you say."

Coffee Time was the last place I wanted to be, but if I missed another shift Gus would fire me, and I still needed to make money for P.J. I'd kept a close watch on him the last two days, but all he ever did was say "Friday" over and over. The very thought of going to school in the morning without his money made me nauseous.

"Okay, Travis," Jordan said, "just remember—" But before he could finish, Koryn's black Jetta streaked by the window. It had just started to rain. Beads of water glistened in Koryn's hair as she hurried through the door.

"Sorry I'm late," she said as she went past the counter. She wore a purple jacket over a T-shirt that ended just above her belly button and big purple shoes with white stars on them. I was jealous of the way she looked at Jordan, but that feeling faded when she said, "Hi, Travis." Before I could say "hi" back she turned the corner to the bathroom.

"So what do you want me to remember?" I asked Jordan.

"Huh? Nothing important."

Although Jordan had said he was going in back, he stayed behind the counter, checking the drip coffee and the bags of espresso in the cabinets. I could have swept the loose beans from under the rubber mats or wiped down the counter, but I didn't. I stood there.

"Did you guys miss me?" Koryn asked, pulling her apron over her head.

"We were waiting breathlessly," Jordan said.

Koryn laughed. I put on a fake smile and noticed that she still wore the purple shoes. Gus would've made her change them but I knew Jordan wouldn't.

"All right," he said, tapping his pen against the clipboard. "Gus is going to check in soon and if I'm not started on this inventory, he'll freak. Holler if you need anything."

"Will do," Koryn said.

Our first customers were a couple of guys in Bard sweatshirts who ordered the coffee of the day. Koryn looked nervous as she served them, and one of the guys smiled at her. "How're you doing?" he said.

"Fine," she said, and that was it. I was surprised, because she was usually so friendly with the customers.

"It's good to see you," he said.

"Hmm, sure."

It seemed like Koryn knew this guy, but she didn't say any more and neither did he. I didn't think much about him, focusing instead on what was in my backpack. I had stayed up until three A.M., drawing sketch after sketch, until my fingers were cramped and my vision was blurry, but I still hadn't captured what I wanted.

We cleaned up for a bit, and Koryn kept looking at the guys, especially the one with the longish hair. The sound of rain on the window was like low-level static. Things were busy enough that we didn't talk much, and that was all right.

When the guys left, Koryn seemed to relax. Then Beth Kittinger walked in, snapping her umbrella shut as she slid through the door.

"Welcome to Coffee Time, ma'am," Koryn said, as though she didn't realize who Beth was.

81

"Hi, Ms. Kittinger," I said, balling up a rag. I wanted to call her "Beth," but it didn't seem right, not with Koryn there.

Why don't you just call her what she is? An off-the-hook hottie.

"Hello, Travis," Beth said. "You're Koryn Walker, aren't you? I'm the new guidance counselor at school."

"Oh, of course, hello."

You got yourself a couple of babes here, Trav-oh. Mmmm-hmmm, deeeee-licious.

Beth smiled, studying the menu and loosening the belt on her long coat, which ended about six inches below her skirt. "So many choices," she said. "I guess I'll have a skim latte, tall please."

"Tall skim latte," Koryn called out. As I began to steam the milk, she leaned over and said, "SMTD." I was glad that she'd remembered, but that feeling was undercut by fear that Beth would see how much I liked Koryn.

Beth asked Koryn questions about school, like what she was taking and who her teachers were. I focused on pouring steamed milk into a paper cup without spilling it.

When I was done, I set the latte on the counter, watching Koryn take Beth's money. Looking down at her open register, Koryn said, "Shit, I'm out of ones. Sorry about that."

I didn't know if she was apologizing for cursing or for having no singles. Beth wasn't fazed. "Quarters are okay," she said. "I can use them for laundry."

As Beth slid quarters into her pocket, Koryn headed for the back room to get more dollar bills. Beth watched me as I took Koryn's place behind the register.

"You two seem to work well together. Do you like being in charge?"

I shrugged, not sure what Beth meant. She must have thought that I was running things, and I didn't correct her.

"Has there been any more trouble at school?" Beth asked, and brought her latte to her lips. I was going to warn her that it might be hot, but she took a long gulp and didn't wince.

"No trouble," I said.

"How about at home?"

"Everything's the same," I said, although I was sure Beth could see how I felt about my parents, the longing I had to shake them and scream, Who's your favorite son now?

Beth nodded and I studied her creamy skin, her probing eyes, her long neck. I imagined jumping over the counter and knocking the latte out of her hand, shoving her against one of the tables, ripping her coat open and pressing my body against her. "Oh, Travis," she'd breathe as the table fell and I pushed her back to the rain-streaked window, her manicured fingers unzipping my pants. . . .

Oh yeah, give it to her. Give it to her good.

While I was daydreaming, Beth had started for the door. She waved and I waved back, watching the drops that pinged against the windows. Beth didn't open her umbrella as she stepped out, as if she didn't mind the rain.

"Hey, Travis, could you do me a favor?" Jordan popped out of the back room, Koryn on his heels. "I need someone to unload last night's delivery. We'll handle things up here."

Normally, I preferred working in the basement, but I didn't want to leave Koryn with Jordan.

You wimp. Don't let him push you around.

"Okay?" Jordan asked, stepping in to take my place behind the register.

It wasn't okay, it wasn't okay at all, but he was my boss and I couldn't say a word.

I'll tell you what you say, you say enough of this bullshit and walk out of here. Say it, you wimp.

But I said nothing, going out of the shop and crossing to an un-marked metal door a couple feet away. Rain drilled me, and in the few seconds it took to get the door opened, I was soaked. Furious, I marched down the concrete stairs and punched in the alarm code at the bottom. I flung the door open on a long basement with no win-dows, and was so angry I almost forgot that the door was on a spring and locked automatically. As it started to swing shut, I groped for its edge, but it whizzed past my fingers and smacked into the frame.

WHAM!

I jiggled the locked knob and kicked at the makeshift doorstop, which was just a piece of torn-off cardboard. "Hey!" I shouted, pounding on the door with my fists. "Hey, let me out!" I banged for several minutes, until my hands were sore, and then I just stood there. My sense of panic was as immediate as the smell of my own wet hair.

Don't be such a wuss, all right? You just need to get your work done and relax.

I took a deep breath and looked around. Metal shelves lined the walls, the gaps in the inventory like holes in a jack-o'-lantern's smile. In the middle of the floor, the delivery boxes were stacked two and three high.

I slid over a box marked coffee filters and picked at the brown tape across the top. The first box wasn't so bad, but by the fifteenth, my fingers hurt and my pinkie was bleeding.

Soon though, I'd finished unpacking all the boxes and there was nothing to do but wait. By then the blood on my finger had crusted to a sticky brown, and though my clothes were damp, my hair was dry. I must've been down there for an hour or two. Wouldn't Jordan have to check on me soon? The darkness pressed in around me, the shelves casting weird shadows. I yanked on the doorknob again, hear-ing it rattle.

"Let me out!"

No answer.

Shivering, I grabbed a wad of napkins from a fresh pack and picked up a pen someone had left on one of the shelves. The ground was cold under my butt as I sat, setting a napkin out before me. I started sketching to distract myself, but I didn't know what to draw.

Draw Jordan, he's the one that got you into this mess.

So I did. On the first napkin, I had myself pushing over one of the massive shelves. Then I drew Jordan buried beneath them, his legs sticking out. On the last napkin I set myself on top of the fallen shelf, Jordan squealing beneath me. I laid the napkins out side by side, like panels in a comic strip.

Don't just draw it. Do it. Show him what you're made of.

I looked at the sketches, then at the shelves behind the door. They weighed far more than I did and were rickety enough that if I shoved them, they would tip right over. Sliding in behind them, I realized I would be out of sight as Jordan entered. I peeked at the spot on the floor where he would need to be standing to get hit. There was already a brown splotch there, a water stain, as though someone had marked it for me.

I felt sure that it was now at least two, even three hours since I'd gone into the basement, but I wasn't frightened. Instead, I grew more calm, knowing all I had to do was wait.

Finally, I heard footsteps, heavy and deliberate. It was Jordan, I knew, wondering why I hadn't come up yet. Hearing the knob turn, I sucked my breath in, tasting stale air. I couldn't see him yet, just heard the scrape of cardboard as he pushed in the makeshift doorstop. Leaning against the shelves, I felt the muscles in my arm strain and heard the creak of rickety metal. Just come right in, I thought, peering around a stack of coffee stirrers.

"Travis, are you in here?" Koryn asked.

She had stopped at the water spot, puzzled. I studied the smooth lines of her face, the way her lips curved up beneath her small nose.

"Travis, is that you?"

Who the hell does she think it is? The big bad wolf?

The shelves creaked again, and I realized I was still leaning against them. As I let go, they groaned back against the wall. "I'm glad you came down," I said, stepping out where she could see me. The cheer in my voice was strained, but I hoped she wouldn't notice.

"Jordan thought maybe you got locked in."

"Yeah, pretty dumb."

"Are you kidding? I almost got locked in here once myself, and I freaked. I hate basements." She looked around uneasily. "We should go up. It's breaktime."

"Breaktime?"

"Well, yeah, it's just past five."

That meant I'd been down there no more than an hour. Was it possible? I looked at Koryn to be sure, but she had her head down, squinting to see the napkins I'd been drawing on. Scooping them into a ball, I felt a twisting dread. "Just passing the time," I said.

As Koryn started for the door, I shoved the napkins in my pocket and inhaled a mix of coffee and perfume, and again I felt the rush I'd had as Beth was walking out of the store. I felt like I had to do something, anything, to change my life and that I had to do it right now. My hand snapped out and my fingers closed around Koryn's wrist, my heart racing as she searched my face. I had no explanation, not one she'd understand, and I wasn't sure what I would say until I heard myself say it.

Just tell her what you want, that's all.

"Koryn, there's something I'd like to ask you."

So go ahead.

"I, uh, I'd like to know if you'd, that is, if you'd . . ."

Spit it out already.

". . . go to the movies with me sometime. Like maybe Friday night."

She tilted her head and I didn't know if she would run out or slap me or just start laughing. A line of coffee powder had streaked her cheek like a skid mark, and I wanted to wipe it away. But I was frozen. I waited for my dreams to be crushed like a spider beneath her hand, and sure enough, Koryn smiled, showing two rows of white teeth and said, "I can't."

My stomach fell and my heart stopped and waves of blackness rolled through me. This was just like that day outside the cafeteria with Taffy—if only I had kept my mouth shut, everything would be fine.

She sucks, you suck, everybody sucks, suck my tasty—

And then she said, "I've got plans Friday. How's Saturday?"

Saturday, I thought, taking a moment to realize she wasn't turning me down, she wasn't blowing me off, she did want to go, and all the tension left my body like air from a punctured tire. I nearly collapsed.

"Saturday's great," I said, following her to the stairs.

I didn't even need to climb the steps, I could practically drift, weightless, like a helium balloon cut from its string, as I rose up the dark stairwell into the light.

Me and Koryn at Coffee Time. Again. I didn't know if I was going to say anything about our "trip." I'd done the research on the internet before school and kept rehearsing what I was going to say. Then I decided maybe it was better to keep quiet.

Koryn seemed kind of off, anyway. I asked her if everything was okay.

"Sure," she said, and smiled tiredly. "This guy I used to know was in here before. Weird, that's all."

The way she said it made me wonder about the guy. But I didn't push it.

By seven, I had to count down the drawers but I told Travis and Koryn to clock out. Travis left first. He kept looking at Koryn before he left, when she wasn't paying attention. Then he put his head down and marched out.

As she watched him go, she said, "He's kind of lonely, isn't he?"

"He has friends."

"But he gets picked on a lot."

"Yeah, P.J.'s kind of hard on him. Travis owes him a bunch of money, you know."

I felt kind of bad about getting the promotion instead of Travis. But maybe he'd want some more hours, make some extra cash. I decided to ask about that when I saw him at school.

"So," Koryn said, as if I'd know what she meant. And I suppose I did. "So you haven't told me where we're going next."

"Savannah," I said.

"Georgia?"

"Yeah, I saw some pictures of it. It looks really amazing, southern gothic you know, and there's all this history. You can see everything, these old plantations, the spot where Eli Whitney invented the cotton gin . . . and best of all, the home of the lady who invented the Girl Scouts."

"Do they sell cookies in the gift shop?" Koryn asked.

I laughed. "I guess we'll find out."

After that we didn't say anything for a minute or so. But it was a good kind of quiet. Then Koryn said, "After Savannah, I think we should go to Nashville."

"Nashville?"

"Well, all around Tennessee. I lived there for a while when I was a kid. I don't remember it much, but I've seen my parents' pictures. Some places are really flat, and then there's these mountains, huge, brown, they go on forever."

"Okay, Nashville."

She nodded. Her eyes were kind of far away. She wasn't just thinking about Tennessee. She was there, and so was I. Then she said: "I better go, before she gets the wrong idea."

Amy was standing in the parking lot. As she came in, Koryn said hi, then bye. Amy half smiled, as if she didn't notice. She looked amazing, like she would for a date.

"Hey, I thought you were supposed to be studying," I said.

"Well, I did study. Then I wanted to see you."

"It's almost your curfew," I said, hedging.

"I told my mother I'd be staying at Taffy's tonight."

"But my mom . . ."

"She'll never know."

"She will," I said.

"Please." Amy pulled her hands up into the sleeves of my old football jacket. They were twice as big as her arms. "You just don't know what it's like," she said, and gave me a serious look. "My mom and dad are fighting again. More than usual."

At least you have a dad, I thought. And Amy started crying,

which meant end of discussion. I held her, then finished my work in
a hurry.

Back home, I snuck Amy up into my room. She lay there so quiet it
was like she was a doll. She stayed until six in the morning. Slipped out
before Mom woke up. Or so I thought.

At breakfast, Mom said, "Amy was here last night, wasn't she?"

I gulped down some juice. "Huh?"

"Be careful with her, Jordan."

Condoms? Was my mom talking to me about birth control
at breakfast?

"Listen, Mom—"

"She's very fragile," Mom said. "Not like you."

"It's fine," I said. "I know what I'm doing."

But I don't know what I'm doing. Right now I don't have the
faintest idea. And I feel bad. About Amy. About Koryn.
About everything.

ON MY WAY TO SCHOOL the next day, I was terrified of having to face P.J. but also high from the thrill of knowing I'd be going out with Koryn. It was just a date, one date, but I already saw how one could lead to the next. In a couple of weeks, I wouldn't even be walking to school. Koryn's Jetta would pull up at my house and I'd run out to meet her and give her a big kiss and then . . .

The fantasy faded as people filed out of the parking lot, jostling and grabbing at each other. I kept a close watch for P.J., but as I passed one of the stone lions by the front steps, it wasn't P.J. that caught my eye. It was Daniel.

He was huddling near the bushes below the front windows with Max Monroe, whose long hair hung down onto his vintage heavy metal T-shirt. I felt a stab of anxiety, unsure why Daniel and Max were together, and then I saw Max pull out some bills. He pressed the money into Daniel's palm and Daniel slapped him on the arm, a friendly gesture, before sliding the cash into the front pocket of his backpack.

I wondered what Daniel had sold Max, and could only come up with one possibility: drugs. I was a little scared. That was a side of Daniel I'd never seen. But even so, I wondered: how much did Max give Daniel? And was the money for me?

I drifted through the front doors, looking over my shoulder. I fumbled open my locker long enough to ball up my jacket and shove it in. It was only fifteen steps to Mrs. Saxon's room and there wasn't much P.J. could do once I got in. But as I closed my locker, my stomach dropped. P.J. was coming up the hall toward me, his beady black eyes big in his face.

My only hope was that with his eyesight, he might not actually see me. He didn't show any sign of recognition, just strutted and swung his arms, muscles rolling under his jacket. I dashed the other way, afraid to turn back, but then I saw Jordan coming from that direction. He called my name and I figured that he and P.J. must be trying to squeeze me between them.

I spun, ran a few steps back toward P.J., and ducked into the bathroom. Racing for one of the open stalls, I bolted the door behind me. If P.J. and Jordan wanted to get me, they'd have to drag me out.

I waited for several minutes, listening to flushing toilets and running water, but no one called my name. Eventually, I heard the belch of the late bell from the hall.

I unlocked the stall to make sure I was alone, catching a glimpse of myself in the mirror. Fear had etched bright red splotches along my cheeks and neck. I combed my hair with my fingers and started for the door when it swung toward me. P.J. entered, looking down at his shoes. I lunged away, banging into the sink so hard I yelped.

His head snapped up. "What the hell're you doing here?" he said, smiling, and I knew then that he hadn't expected to find me. There'd been no plan with Jordan, no attempt to trap me. I'd trapped myself.

"Now where's my money?" P.J. asked.

As I pulled out the envelope I'd prepared, a couple of nickels fell out and clattered against the floor. One rolled into a urinal, the other circled P.J.'s heavy white sneaker.

"What'd you do, break open your piggy bank?"

He nearly ripped the envelope from my fingers. Yanking out the bills, which were as worn as old cotton, he held them in his hand as if he could count by weight. "This isn't the full three hundred."

"You said one fifty to start."

"It's not one fifty either. How much is it?"

Why doesn't he use his fingers and count it for himself?

"It's all I've got."

"Get more!" P.J. screamed, stabbing a finger at my chest. "You'd better do it, and do it fast."

I heard the door open behind me, and figured that whoever it was would see what was going on and back right out. But there was no sound of the door closing, as if whoever it was had stayed right there, and then I heard Daniel: "How much more?"

P.J. froze, looking as surprised as I felt, but he recovered quickly. "What the hell's it matter to you?"

I half turned, not wanting to take my eyes off P.J., and saw Daniel's reflection appear in the mirror. "You want your money or not?" Daniel asked. Then to me: "How much are you short?"

"Answer him, you retard," P.J. said.

"I've got seventy-three dollars and, uh, eleven cents. So I guess that's about sixty-seven, um, sixty-six—"

"I want another eighty bucks," P.J. said. "Plus the other one fifty by Monday."

Eighty? I thought. That wasn't fair, not fair at all. But Daniel looked at P.J. and nodded. "Eighty now and another one fifty and that's it," he said. "No more bullshit."

"No more bullshit," P.J. agreed.

Daniel reached in his pocket and counted out three twenty dollar bills, two fives, and a bunch of ones. As Daniel started to hand the money over, P.J. grabbed for it, but Daniel yanked the bills away as if he were playing rough with a new puppy. He flung the money into the air, green paper raining down around us.

Before I could ask what he was doing, he grabbed my arm and pulled me to the door. P.J. started to chase after us, then looked back at the bills raining down, landing in the sinks and on the windowsill. "You assholes," he said, "I don't care how much is here, you're dead, dead as a—"

But we didn't hear the rest as we ducked out into the hall, running toward Mrs. Saxon's room.

"You shouldn't have done that," I said.

"What, I should've just handed it over? He would've beaten the crap out of us *and* taken all my money."

I wanted to argue, but I couldn't. It was a scenario I could imagine all too easily.

"Besides, I've got to put the rest back in the freezer," Daniel said.

"The freezer?"

"My parents keep a few hundred in there for emergencies. It's fine, as long as I replace it in a couple of weeks."

Bullshit, I thought. I knew Daniel hadn't gotten the money from his freezer, and I wanted to tell him that. But I let it go.

Still, my discomfort must have showed on my face. Daniel looked at me sympathetically. This was, I realized, the first time he misunderstood what I was thinking, but not the last. "Don't you worry about Monday," he said. "P.J.'ll get exactly what he deserves."

On my way to lunch, I passed Ross and Moira standing by an open locker. Moira's face was red, the way it got when she'd been running around during gym, and Ross looked pale, his lip stuck out as though he was trying not to cry.

"What happened?" I asked. I'd spent the entire morning dodging P.J., and I didn't like the idea of standing in the hallway, exposed. But Ross and Moira were miserable. He put a hand on the edge of his locker door as if to hold himself up. She squeezed his forearm, then looked at me.

"If this is some kind of joke, nobody's laughing," she said.

"No shit," I said. "What's going on?"

"There's a problem," Ross said, a slight tremor in his voice.

"Hey guys," Daniel said, elbowing me from behind.

"Ross's GameBox is missing," Moira said.

"What does that have to do with us?" I asked. But then I remembered the wad of money Daniel had taken from Max Monroe. That was no drug deal.

"Never mind," Ross said miserably, and slammed his locker door. His hand made a hollow sound against the metal.

Other kids pushed past us from both directions, some of them banging me with their backpacks. I moved in closer to Ross and Moira so that I wouldn't get trampled. Daniel stayed where he was, but then everyone just seemed to walk around him.

"Bullshit," Moira said. "I know you did this." Her eyes flicked from me to Daniel. "Now give it back and we'll forget it."

"What are you talking about?" Daniel said. "I don't even know Ross's locker combination."

"You've seen him use it," Moira said.

"So have a million other people. Maybe one of them took his stupid game thing." Daniel's voice was spiked with annoyance, and if I didn't know better, I would've believed he was innocent.

"I didn't take it either," I said, feeling equally annoyed.

"Please, Travis." Although Moira looked close to tears, there was something almost pretty in her soft face. I wanted to tell her that yes, we'd get Ross's GameBox back, but I couldn't see how.

"I told you," Ross said. "It wasn't them."

"Yes, it was." Moira's voice was so shrill that several people looked over. "I saw the way you were looking at it," she told me. "You wanted it, and you had Daniel steal it for you. Or you took it for yourself. Or I don't know."

Now I was angry. If Moira or Ross had just given me some

money in the first place, this never would've happened. But they'd been selfish, and Daniel was the only one willing to stand up for me. I wanted to tell them that.

Instead I said, "I'm the best friend you guys have, your only friend really, and you accuse me of doing something like this when the whole school is full of shitheads who could've taken your stupid video game? What about P.J.? He was looking at it too."

Ross was practically sputtering. "Listen, Travis, you know Moira—"

"No, you listen. You stay the hell away from me." I nodded at Daniel. "From us."

I started off down the hall, which was now almost empty. It took Daniel about ten seconds to catch up to me. When he did, the first thing I said was: "So why'd you lie about stealing the GameBox?"

His eyes were more alert than they'd been. "Moira wouldn't exactly give me a medal, would she?"

"I meant to me."

"I didn't want you to have to be a part of it."

"Well, I am a part of it," I said. "I saw you and Max. And I wish you hadn't done that."

"Do you wish P.J. had drilled you in the dome a few times? You needed the money, right? Besides, Ross'll just buy himself a new one."

Forget Moira and Ross. You don't need them. You don't need anyone.

Except Daniel, I thought, as we came to the back of the lunch line. I stopped behind the last person even as Daniel kept walking. "Where are you going?" I asked.

"Not hungry," he said, heading straight into the cafeteria. I watched as he went past our usual table and stopped where he'd sat alone the first week of school. A lump formed in my throat even as something started to squirm in my belly.

After waiting in line, I walked right by Ross and Moira, keeping my head up and my arms out, the tray balanced steadily as I made my way to Daniel. I sat with my back to my friends and to P.J. I had the sense that all three of them were watching me, but resisted the urge to turn.

I pulled out my sketch pad, but I didn't feel much like drawing. I wasn't too interested in my burger either.

As I picked at my burger, Daniel said, "This is a special occasion. You know what you ought to do to celebrate?"

I knew, all right. I unfolded the slip of paper from my pocket and fished a pen out of my backpack. I focused on the thin blue lines that ran along the page, remembering how long I had known Moira and Ross, how much we'd been through together. I recalled the night after Richie's funeral, one of the few times we were all at my house. The adults had gathered in the living room, and I hid out with Ross and Moira in my bedroom, staring at the wall that separated Richie's room and mine. I felt a hand on each shoulder, but I didn't know if it was Ross or Moira who had touched me, or both of them. "I know how bad you feel, but we're here for you," Moira said. "We'll always be here. Forever."

Thinking about twelve years of friendship and the weight of broken promises, I studied Daniel. His eyes were unrelenting, his face as hard as the linoleum floor. Wherever I looked his eyes seemed to follow, so I turned back to the list.

"What are you waiting for?" he asked. "You trying to protect those so-called friends of yours? From what? If it was up to them, P.J. would've beaten you senseless. They don't care about you, Travis. They never have. I thought you'd see that by now."

I did see that, and what's more I saw how Moira had betrayed me. If she had something against Daniel, fine, but she'd known *me* her whole life, and still she accused me of being a thief. I'd never stolen anything from her, even though I could have done it a hundred times, a thousand even. She cared more about the things she owned than she did about me, and I hated her for it.

Tears sprung to my eyes, but I wouldn't let them come. I wasn't going to show any weakness, just do what I had to do. I put Moira's name on the list, writing so hard the pen tore through the paper. Daniel looked pleased.

New York State Police
interview with Taffy Martin

DET. UPSHAW: Can you tell me why P.J. was so fixated
on Travis?

TAFFY: P.J. didn't hate him or anything. It's just that Travis
was easy to pick on. He never fought back, never said
anything, just went along.

DET. UPSHAW: So P.J. kept on taunting him?

TAFFY: P.J. was upset about his windshield, that's how it
started. He wanted his money. And yeah, he got kind of
pushy about it. But he wasn't trying to hurt Travis. He
was just having some fun. If Travis had stood up for
himself, really said, listen, I'm not going to take this
anymore, P.J. would've eased up on him, I know he would.
(SOUNDS OF CRYING) I'm not trying to make excuses but ... oh
God, he just didn't know anything like this could happen.
Not here, not to us.

I SPENT THREE HOURS getting ready for my date with Koryn. I put shirts on and took them off and kept sniffing my armpits to make sure my deodorant was really working. I'd hoped to go out shooting with Daniel that afternoon, but he had to see his grandmother in the hospital again.

"When's she going to get out?" I asked.

"Maybe never. The doctors can't figure out what's wrong with her. First it was her lungs, now they say it's her heart. I just wish she'd check out for good."

"Daniel!"

"Well, I do. She's always been kind of nasty. Nothing's ever good enough for her, and she looks down on everyone, especially me. I won't miss her, that's for sure."

We spent another hour on the phone, Daniel giving me last minute advice for my date. I listened carefully, taking in every bit of information, because I wanted everything to be perfect. But I was terrified that I would somehow mess it up.

Since Koryn and I were meeting at the mall, I needed my father to drive me there. We didn't talk much on the way. As we rolled onto the dark road on the far side of the Kingston Bridge, music filled the emptiness. Power 106 was doing an all nineties hour, the Genesis song "You're No Son of Mine" giving way to the Cranberries' "I Can't Be With You."

"Richie used to love this song," I said, surprised by the sudden announcement.

"Huh" was all my father said. I'd half expected some kind of explosion, like when my mother mentioned Richie at dinner.

"How come you never talk about Richie, Dad?"

"I'm not sure what you'd like me to say about him, Travis."

"You could talk about the things you used to do with him, I guess."

Like kiss his ass, right, Trav-oh?

"I suppose I could, but why should I? Richie was a very lucky young man. He had the kind of chances most people never get in life, and he wasted them. He wasted everything he ever had." My father's voice was raspy, the way it sometimes got when he'd had too much beer.

"Not everything," I said. Without Richie there to stand up for himself, I felt like I owed it to him to provide a defense. "Richie did a lot of good things."

"He could've done a whole hell of a lot more if he hadn't—" But my father cut himself off before he got to the point he was driving at. "Travis, I know you idolize Richie, and why not? He was your big brother. But in spite of what your mother thinks, he was no goddamn saint. He was cocky, self-absorbed, vain—of course, I have no one to blame but myself . . . and your mother. She spoiled that boy rotten from the moment he was born. In her eyes, he was just a little angel who could never do any wrong."

I shook my head, anger spreading across my skin like water poured on glass. But I continued to listen, saying nothing.

"For most of his life, everything came easy. It was all handed right down on a silver platter. Well, the world isn't like that. You've got to work too hard for too little and settle for what you get. That's how it is, Travis, and Richie couldn't deal with it. He thought he was special or something. Well, I guess the world showed him."

"Bullshit," I said.

My father looked over, surprised. He pulled over at the start of the access road below the mall.

"Richie worked hard, and he was smart, and he could've done something with his life. You're the one that tried to throw him out of the house, you're the one that wouldn't help him. It's your goddamn fault he killed himself."

My father's eyes narrowed. "Your mother's feeding you her goddamn shrink talk, isn't she? That woman doesn't have enough sense to—"

"She didn't do anything!" I erupted. "I can think for myself. And I think you're full of shit. Richie always knew it, and so do I."

My father looked so stunned that he didn't respond. I didn't give him a chance to, anyway, just jumped out of the car and started up the hill to the mall.

I was already running behind schedule and now I'd really be late. Part of me wanted to run away, just escape, but where would I go? Not home. And Daniel was away. Besides, my date with Koryn was too important to just give up on. But my heart was thundering and my thoughts were cycling at a hundred miles an hour. I'd never stood up to my father before, and it felt both exciting and terrifying at the same time.

As I climbed the dark road, headlights slashed toward me. I was only half surprised to see that the approaching car looked like P.J.'s Taurus. I couldn't make out the driver's face but I noticed there was no crack in the windshield. As the Taurus angled out of sight, I moved with new purpose.

It took me five minutes to get to the parking lot, and another five to find the car. It was wedged into a compact space between a minivan and a Civic. The Shadwell Sharks bumper sticker with KICK ASS written on it was as obvious as a tattoo. The exterior gleamed under the parking lot lights, as if P.J. had spent all day waxing it.

The windshield was indeed flawless. Seeing it, I thought: I'm free, P.J. took the money Daniel and I gave him and fixed his windshield and I'm free. I wiped away what might have been sweat or maybe a tear and smiled as I crossed to the mall.

The wind was pleasantly cool and the falling leaves were like confetti. I suddenly knew, just knew, that everything was going to be all right.

And then I heard, "What'd you do to my car this time?"

P.J. stepped out from the behind the mall's glass doors, as if he'd been waiting for me. A couple of kids whose faces I knew from school—freshmen or sophomores at most—stood by the next set of doors, getting in the last puffs of their cigarettes.

"You fixed it," I said. "We're square."

"You're square, all right, you stupid prick."

"Your windshield's fixed." I couldn't keep the enthusiasm out of my voice, even though I knew he would seize on it.

"Yeah, it's fixed. But I still owe the dude at the body shop another hundred and fifty bones. And you better have it Monday. Because unlike you, I pay my debts."

I studied him and realized something instantly: he was lying. Maybe it was the glint in his eyes or the way he shifted his weight from one foot to the other. But I was sure he'd gotten the windshield fixed for the money I'd already given him. He only wanted the rest for himself.

"No," I said, hating the whine I heard in my voice. "We're even."

"Even-steven," P.J. said, laughing. Then, suddenly noticing my stiff button-down shirt: "Hey, what're you all dressed up for?"

"Nothing."

"You got a date or something?"

Before I could reply, Taffy stepped out of the mall, tapping her wrist as though she had a watch on. "Honey, we're going to be late for the movie."

"Hey, Taff, I think Travis has a hot date. Only I can't imagine who the hell would go out with him."

She tugged at P.J.'s arm. "Come on."

"We were finished anyway, weren't we, Travis?"

Oh, he's finished all right. We're going to finish him even-steven, just the way he likes.

"Sure," I said.

After they left I waited there for a minute or two, even though I was late already, just to give them a head start. Finally, stomach cramped with anxiety, I started down the mall corridor. The store windows were full of dummies dressed in hip-hugging jeans and decorated with huge jack-o'-lanterns. I nearly choked on the too-hot air.

And then I saw Koryn below the glowing marquee of the movie theater. She wore jeans with a blue and red banner around the cuffs and a pink sweater that looked as soft as teddy bear fur. The panic disappeared like a noose that had been cut away.

"I wasn't sure you were going to make it," Koryn said.

"Sorry I'm late. I ran into someone on the way."

As I moved toward the ticket line, I pulled out the twenty-dollar bill I'd stashed in my front pocket, money Daniel had given me. There was one more twenty in my wallet, along with a condom, another present from Daniel. "You probably won't need it," he'd said, "but better safe than sorry."

I looked back at Koryn, but she stayed where she was. "Oh, I've already got my ticket."

"Great," I said. Shit. Daniel had told me that it was absolutely crucial—"A-1 important"—to buy the tickets for both of us. "Only dweebs let a girl go Dutch," he'd said.

But there I was in line, alone, behind a couple that could barely stop making out long enough to hand over their money. Inside, I bought popcorn for myself and Koryn got a Diet Coke and we didn't talk again until we were in our seats. Even then, every attempt at conversation dribbled out quickly.

The movie was a comedy, but it was impossible to focus on the action with Koryn so close. I felt her breath on my cheek and thought she must be turned my way, but when I glanced over she was staring at the screen. I dug my fingers into the popcorn, chewing quietly.

"When the movie starts, she's going to want you to hold her hand," Daniel had told me. "Just don't wait too long to go for it."

Twenty minutes in, the main character was starting to show his loveably demented side, and I was ready to make my first move. Just as I lifted my hand, Koryn erupted in a burst of laughter, and I joined in half a second later. There was a lull after that and I returned my attention to her, even as I felt a swarm of panic. The movie would be over before I knew it.

Then stop screwing around already.

Inhaling sharply, I reached over and let my right hand find her left, which rested on her thigh. I felt the smoothness of her fingers and the roughness of her jeans. For a second I didn't breathe and then Koryn's hand shifted. She grabbed my fingers and set them on the armrest between us, putting her own hand on top. It stayed for three seconds, then moved away.

I thought of one of the last things Daniel had said on the phone. "Don't worry if she's a little cool at first. All girls play hard to get. You just have to keep pushing them until they give you what you want. They want it as much as you do, believe me."

Maybe Daniel was right and Koryn was playing games, but I didn't have the guts to reach for her again. Instead, I sat there miserably, wishing the movie would just be over. Nothing was funny to me but I matched Koryn's laughter chuckle for chuckle. Mine was hollow, but she didn't seem to notice.

When the credits began to roll, I wondered if she would say something about me trying to hold her hand. She didn't. Instead she talked about her favorite scenes and I tried to remember those parts of the movie. But I couldn't.

"I'm glad you asked me to go out, Travis."

"Me too."

I couldn't stop thinking about how she'd rejected me. Daniel knew more about situations like this than I did, and his instructions were clear: I just had to push a little to get what I wanted.

She wants it too, wants it bad.

"So how did you get here?" she asked.

I'd been dreading that question, almost as much as I'd dreaded having to call my father to come get me. "I walked," I said.

"All the way?" She raised her eyebrows at me, probably thinking about how far that was. "So you want a ride home? I mean, unless you like to walk."

It sounded like she was making fun of me, but she was smiling. I felt light-headed and nauseous. Noise swelled around us as we walked out of the mall. The night wind cut my skin and I wished I had worn a heavier jacket. I pressed my lips tight, afraid my teeth would start chattering.

Koryn's Jetta sat by itself. It gleamed on the outside and was plush within. I settled in the passenger seat as she started the engine. This is my chance, I thought, listening to the rumble from beneath the hood. The windows steamed up quickly and Koryn flicked on the defogger.

C'mon now, you know what she wants. Give it to her.

As Koryn brought her hand to the steering wheel, I leaned over and kissed her. The gearshift jabbed my side and I felt the pressure of the wheel behind me. Koryn's lips had that too-sweet flavor of Diet Coke and the car smelled like mints and perfume. Pushing my tongue out, I felt the inside of Koryn's mouth and brought one of my hands up into her hair. Koryn was calling my name, first once and then again, and there was the pressure of her body as she met mine, and all I could think about was that girl-flesh and how hot it would feel against me.

"*TRAVIS!*"

She'd been saying my name for fifteen or twenty seconds, maybe even shouting it, but this was only a half step from a scream. "Goddammit, Travis," she said, as I pulled my mouth away, her hand shoving me in the chest. My leg had gone numb from the gearshift.

"Travis, I said stop!"

She wiped at her mouth as though she'd tasted sour milk. Her pretty face was ruined by eyes closed to slits and lips that looked nearly white.

"I'm sorry," I said.

"What the hell are you doing?" she snapped. Then more calmly: "Travis, I thought you were my friend."

There was something about that word. It sounded off-key, like a misplayed note in a beautiful song.

"I am," I said, the blood pounding through my temples.

"I don't see how friends . . ." But whatever she'd been about to say, she stopped herself. "Maybe I shouldn't have gone out with you tonight."

"Don't say that." I turned to the fogged glass and grabbed the door handle. I wanted to say more but my throat had tightened up so I left the car and just ran, feeling detached from my own body, the cold seeping under someone else's skin, the snot dripping from someone else's nose.

You're a loser, Trav-oh, a goddamn loser, can't even go on a date without screwing it up.

A moment later, the red circles of Koryn's taillights buzzed across the lot, and soon they were lost in the night. This time I really did walk, six miles through the cold and the dark, and by the last stretch of road I couldn't feel my hands or face. All I kept thinking was that in a few hours it would be morning and I'd be able to call Daniel and tell him what had happened.

He would know what to do.

He would know how to fix everything.

Weird night. Super weird. Not bad. Good, really, but strange.

Amy went to her aunt's in Beacon for the weekend. I was on my own. Mom was in the living room, reading. I watched ESPN, Braves and Mets. The Mets were kicking ass, and I had a big bag of onion—garlic chips. Life was good.

P.J. stopped by on his way back from the movies. He'd just dropped off Taffy and had to get home soon. We talked about the baseball game and some school stuff. Then he said, "Hey, did I leave my hat over here?"

"What hat?"

"You know, my team hat."

The only hat I had was mine. I told him so.

"It just pisses me off. I had it at school yesterday, at least I thought I did. I could swear I saw it in my locker, but when I left yesterday it was gone."

I listened to him go on about the hat, but I didn't get too excited. He went through three or four of them a year. Every year.

A few minutes later, the doorbell rang. I figured it was P.J. again. Probably telling me he'd found his hat in the car.

Then I got the door. Total surprise.

It was Koryn. She looked like hell. Her cheeks were all red. Hair messed up.

I asked her what was going on.

"I'm fine," Koryn said. But she didn't look fine.

I led her up to the bathroom and gave her a towel. Let her wash up. When she came out, she looked better. She was almost smiling, but didn't seem to mean it.

"I shouldn't have come," she said. "I better go."

"Please, don't."

She looked at the stairs.

"Tell me what happened," I said.

"It doesn't matter. I made a mistake and I feel stupid and I'd rather not talk about it."

"Okay, but I want you to stay."

She turned to me. I had no idea what she was going to say. I had a feeling it was "no."

My mother's shadow was at the bottom of the steps.

"Everything's okay," I called out.

The shadow disappeared. I led the way to my room, and Koryn followed. I left the door open a little. Koryn looked around. Picked up books. *Journey to the Center of the Earth. The Grapes of Wrath. The Stand.* Flipping pages, she said, "Pendleton, Oregon."

"Okay," I said, waiting.

"That's where I used to live, before we moved here. My parents taught at Pendleton College. It's only about six hours from Great Falls, Montana. I still have a couple of friends there, we could stay with them. It's real pretty."

"Okay," I said again. Looked at her. Really looked. And our so-called trip didn't feel like such a joke anymore.

I didn't mean to kiss her. It just happened. Our faces were so close. Her lips were soft and the kiss was short. She ended it.

"I'm sorry," I said. But I wasn't.

She started to pull her jacket on.

"You don't have to—"

"Yes, I do," she said.

"No. Really."

She shook her head. "Amy's going to hate me, more than she does already. But not as much as I hate myself."

"Koryn, listen to me—"

"Jordan, I can't. Good night."

She touched my cheek as she left. I can still feel her lips. Writing it down, it doesn't seem real. By the way, just watched SportsCenter. Braves rallied. Mets lost.

3 DAYS TO GO

WHEN I WENT TO DANIEL'S house on Sunday afternoon, Mr. Pulver answered the door. I'd never seen him before and if I'd met him on the street I never would've figured him for Daniel's father. He had broad shoulders like my father but he wasn't tall and there was little sign that any of his fat had ever been muscle. He didn't look like a CEO but he sounded like one. "Craig Pulver. It's good to meet you, young man," he boomed.

"I'm Travis."

His handshake hurt my fingers. "I know. My son thinks quite highly of you. And like me, he doesn't impress easily."

"Thanks, I guess."

"But don't you get him into any trouble, all right?"

"Sir?"

"Because you'll have to answer to me if you do. Both of you."

"Ummm—"

"You understand me, Travis?"

I looked at Craig Pulver's face to try to figure out whether he was serious. I couldn't tell until he broke into a broad smile, and even then I wasn't sure. "Don't you kids have a sense of humor anymore? Come on, let's go find—"

"Travis." Daniel padded over in his bare feet, then nodded at the stairs.

"Don't make too much noise up there," Craig Pulver said. "I don't want you to bother your mother."

With his back to his father, Daniel rolled his eyes. I started to follow him, but froze when Craig's heavy hand shot out, clamping tightly on Daniel's shoulder. "I'm serious, Danny."

"I know," Daniel said.

As we left his father, I said, "How come your mom didn't go to the hospital today?"

"A migraine. She can't do anything when she gets one of those."

"But your grandmother's still sick?"

"Oh, yeah, sick in the head. She's really bad all of a sudden, can't remember who anybody is. Even my mother's saying it'd be better if she just died."

He kept his voice low as we passed the closed door of his parents' bedroom. In his room, I noticed that some of the cardboard boxes were gone. The walls weren't totally bare anymore either. A poster from *The Matrix* was stuck to the wall above Daniel's TV with black pushpins. Just like mine.

"I just got a bunch of new DVDs," he said. "You want to eyeball something?"

We put on *The Matrix* but kept the volume low. It was just as hard to focus on what I was watching as it had been the night before, only for different reasons. I kept replaying the scene with Koryn in the car again and again, like a mental DVD on an endless loop. I'd told Daniel about it on the phone earlier, and he'd said it wasn't my fault. "She was just being a goddamn tease. There's nothing you could've done. We'll forget all about her."

But I couldn't forget about what had happened with her or with my father either. I hadn't seen my parents until that morning. My father was so engrossed in his coffee and his newspaper that he didn't say a word. Finally, my mother asked, "Did you have fun with your friends last night?" I'd told her I was going out with Ross and Moira.

"It was fine," I said. My father grunted and announced that he had to go into work, even though it was Sunday, and he abruptly left the table.

But after breakfast, I found myself face to face with him in the hallway. He said, "I didn't tell your mother about last night, and I don't intend to. But you'd better watch what you say and do from now on. You understand me?"

You watch yourself, you goddamn drunk, you worthless—

But I'd tuned the voice out and nodded, too scared to challenge my father again.

Across the room, I saw that Daniel wasn't watching the movie any more than I was. He was studying me. Once he had my attention, he crossed to the doorway. I followed him down the hall, a tingle of fear in my legs as he opened the door to his parents' room. From downstairs, I heard his father's voice. "No, I haven't seen it in days, Mrs. Barker . . . Sorry, haven't seen *him*, of course . . . Yes, I'll ask my wife. Daniel too."

"What're you doing?" I hissed as Daniel glided into his parents' room. His mother looked almost as faint as a mirage. Her shirt had pulled up a little, showing the pink elastic of her underwear. Daniel reached for the nightstand next to the bed, sliding out the top drawer. It sounded as loud as the screech of a car's brakes, but his mother didn't stir.

Daniel pulled out the Beretta.

"Daniel," I whispered, and his mother's head twitched. I waited for her to jump up and cry, "What're you doing in here?" but her cheek settled back on the pillow. Her breathing was steady as Daniel reached past her again, pulling out the box of bullets. He slid it into his pocket.

Edging for the door, I expected to see Daniel right behind me, but he was still by the bed. He raised the Beretta, putting the barrel into the wisps of blond hair that curled away from his mother's head.

"Jesus, Daniel—" I started.

He put a finger to his lips like Principal McCarthy in the school library, only he didn't make a sound.

I was terrified. Not just that his mother would wake up, but that Daniel would pull the trigger. The gun shouldn't have been loaded, but what if it was?

"Danny?" Madeline said, squirming on the blankets.

He touched her face with his free hand, the gun still pointed at her. "It's okay, Mom, go back to sleep."

"Mmmm" was her response. I took an involuntary step to the door, the hall light hurting my eyes. Madeline drew one hand up near her face and laid it on the pillow, just missing the gun.

"Sleep tight," Daniel said, his voice softer than a feather, and backed away.

He closed the door behind us without a sound. From below, I heard his father again. "Yes, Mrs. Barker, I know you're concerned," Craig Pulver said. "But there's nothing else I can do, I'm afraid. Good-bye."

"Come on," Daniel said, sliding the gun into the front of his jeans and covering it with his shirt. "Let's go."

Downstairs, Daniel's father held the phone receiver at his side, tapping it against his thigh impatiently. "That was Mrs. Barker again," he said. "She's worried about her dog."

"I haven't seen that old mutt," Daniel said.

"Of course not. It probably just started chasing a squirrel and ran off." Craig scratched at his scalp, looking at Daniel from the corners of his eyes as if searching for something he couldn't see head-on.

"Probably," Daniel said. "We're going out."

"All right." Craig looked at me as he said it, as if my face might reveal something Daniel's hadn't. But I just nodded and smiled.

My sneakers crunched on dead leaves and fallen branches as we plowed through the still woods. I curled and uncurled my fingers to keep the blood moving, watching the silver slopes of the mountains disappear beyond the tree line. Next door to Daniel's house, a wrinkled face peeked out the window, and then a hand slipped a pair of glasses into place on a jagged nose. It was the woman I'd seen out with her dog, Alfie, a few nights before.

"Is that Mrs. Barker?" I asked.

"Mrs. Bonkers is more like it. She's a regular fruit loop." Daniel started walking a little faster, or maybe I was going slower, because he was soon half a dozen yards ahead. "Are you coming or what?"

"Your mom might've caught us," I said, hurrying after him.

"She didn't."

"What about your dad? What if he notices the gun's missing?"

"He won't."

I'd forgotten about Koryn, at least for a little while. But as I walked the memories came flooding back, along with the image of P.J.'s car and that perfect windshield.

"You've got to stop thinking about her," Daniel said.

"I'm not."

"What, then?" He studied me. "P.J.?"

"He still wants his money tomorrow."

"We'll take care of it. Meet me at school early tomorrow, eight o'clock, and you won't have any more problems with him. I promise." Part of me wanted to know what he had in mind, but another part was so tired of worrying that I decided to trust him.

"Now forget school, dude, 'cause we're gonna have some fun," he said.

I nodded, willing to try. "But we don't even have any cans."

"No shit, Sherlock. Guess we'll need a different target."

Instead of going straight up the incline again, Daniel veered off through the pine trees. In the distance, the tall stalks of a cornfield quivered. About fifty yards short of the cornfield, narrow lumps of raw earth were arranged like a series of speed bumps.

As we got closer, I saw that beyond the empty rows were dozens of pumpkins with long, ropy vines stringing them together. Some were nearly perfect, while others were bloated and misshapen.

"We need targets, right?" Daniel asked.

I broke into an unexpected grin. "But we can't take these."

"There's a million of them. They won't miss three or four."

We climbed around in the rows, until Daniel hefted a pumpkin about the size of a basketball. I found one that was as big as a Thanksgiving turkey. Its orange skin was even, the ridges of pumpkin flesh lightly crusted with dirt. The vine along the top pulled away easily, but when I rolled the pumpkin into my arms, I felt a mushy spot along the bottom.

"Shit," I said, letting it roll away.

Daniel laughed. "Come on already. We haven't got all day."

I quickly settled on a couple of midsized pumpkins and carried them in my arms. When we arrived at the spot where we'd shot the cans, I almost didn't recognize it, since we'd come from the opposite direction.

"Let's set 'em up," he said.

We lined up the four pumpkins on a mostly-flat boulder in descending size order. Daniel had the biggest and the smallest, and mine fit in between. I looked for the line Daniel had drawn in the dirt the other day, but I couldn't find it. He used his heel to make another, then pulled the gun out of his waistband and loaded slugs into the magazine.

Although I was excited to shoot again, I kept thinking about Koryn. I knew that she hated me and she'd never talk to me and I was miserable. I wanted to curl up in the dirt and rot like one of those old pumpkins. Then again, I'd been waiting all week for the chance to go shooting again, and I wasn't going to let anything ruin it, even her.

"Go ahead," Daniel said. "You first."

The weight of the gun felt just right this time, the metal cool against my palm. I ran two fingers along the barrel, and settled my sneakers so that my toes were half an inch behind the dirt line. Then I raised my arms and extended them like Daniel had showed me. I settled the sights on the largest pumpkin, which was caught in a wedge of sunlight.

"Wait," Daniel said. "We should try something different."

"Different how?"

"Let's stand sideways, then spin and shoot. Like in the movies."

"Yeah, right. Why don't we just put blindfolds on too?"

But I lowered the gun and turned sideways, facing the mountains, where the sun had turned the silver peaks almost black.

"Okay, get ready," Daniel said. "On the count of three."

I licked my lips and again thought of Koryn, her eyes and lips seething with anger and hurt.

"One . . ."

You ought to teach her a lesson.

"Two."

The kind she won't forget.

"Three."

Oh yeah, it'll be easy.

I whirled in what was probably the most graceful motion I'd ever made, body spinning like a top, both arms coming up in a single fluid motion. The gun rose in my vision and the pumpkins were no more than three orange blurs, so I just squeezed the trigger once, twice, three times, my heart bobbing in my throat and my chest full of air, the sound of the shots crackling like thunder.

When I looked off to the side, Daniel's mouth was open, his chest heaving. He must've been laughing, but my ears were ringing so bad I couldn't hear. I hadn't hit a single pumpkin.

What's he laughing at? Go ahead, show that loser what you can REALLY *do.*

Daniel started toward me, his hand extended for the gun, but I was so pissed that I turned away and snapped my arms back into position, elbows locked, gun straight out, and focused all my attention down the sights at the smallest pumpkin. I pulled the trigger. The explosion happened almost instantly, the orange skin erupting as though there were a firecracker in it.

When I felt Daniel's hand clap my shoulder, I nearly jumped.

"You'd better put the safety on, Rambo. Before you blast your foot off."

I examined the ruins of the pumpkin. Pieces of rind and seeds had spread across the boulder. The biggest piece, a chunk the size and shape of a candy dish, lay on its side. I picked it up, touching the spongy softness within.

"My turn," Daniel said.

He started sideways and spun, but he couldn't hit anything either. When I tried it that way a second time, I managed to nick the biggest pumpkin's stem. After that, we gave up on the spin move and shot head-on, and then I blasted that pumpkin clean off the boulder. Daniel took care of one middle pumpkin, which left me the other. I was ready to nail it when Daniel said that he wanted to bring it home instead.

He held the pumpkin as I slipped the gun into my jacket pocket. I felt so happy that I was sure I could never be miserable again, so strong that I knew I could stand up to P.J. and anyone else who crossed me. The air was cooling and the sky was darkening but the woods felt brighter than before. I kept putting my hand in my pocket, finding the warm barrel, and I was so distracted that I almost didn't see the shape through the woods.

When I did, I froze.

It was low to the ground and grayish-black. Daniel kept going straight but I headed for the creature sprawled against the base of the tree.

As I got closer, I saw that the gray fur was matted with dried blood. A piece of rope circled its neck, the other end tied to the tree. There was also a blue collar with two gold tags in the shape of bones hanging from its neck. I didn't need to read it to know that the name engraved there was Alfie.

The animal's eyes were just empty holes, pinkish-gray matter showing through the deep caverns, and its mouth was pulled together like an old wound, teeth barely visible. The dog had been dead for a couple days, and the reek of its flesh was so strong that I spun away, puking into a pile of leaves.

C'mon, pull yourself together. You're acting like a goddamn girl.

"You all right?" Daniel asked.

Wiping the back of my mouth with my hand, I nodded. "That's your neighbor's dog."

"Sure is," Daniel said. "It looks like someone tied it up out here and let it starve to death. Or maybe the animals got it first."

"Oh man," I said. "Who would do something like that?"

I thought of poor Simms as we dragged him into the vet's office and shuddered.

"I don't know," Daniel said. "I never liked that dog, anyway."

I looked at him then as if I'd never quite seen him before. There was nothing unusual about him though. His eyes were bright, his hair hanging down into them, his hands shoved in the pockets of his coat.

"Did you . . . do this?" I asked.

"No," Daniel said, as if insulted. "Would I waste my time with some stupid dog? Besides, that's sick."

"You're damn right it's sick," I said. "Hurting a poor defense-less animal."

"And I told you I didn't do it. Whoever did though, they'd have to be pretty strong to drag that dog all the way out here. That mutt was pretty big, you know."

He took a couple of steps forward and froze, staring at something about six feet from the dog's body. I looked over at what he'd seen: blue cloth showing through some fallen leaves. But what was it? I picked the object up, turned it over in my hands. It was a well-worn Shadwell Sharks baseball cap.

You know what that means, don't you, Trav-oh?

"Jesus," Daniel said.

"So it's got to be someone from school."

"Not just someone." Daniel took the cap from me and flung it back onto the ground as if it were diseased. "I think you know who it was. There's only one person mean enough to do something like this, and that's P.J."

What a sicko! Someone ought to tie HIM up, starve HIM, see how HE likes it.

I glanced back at the dead animal and felt my gorge rising again. My arms broke out in goose bumps, and not just from the cold. I closed my fingers around the grip of the gun in a protective instinct. I knew P.J. was cruel, but I'd never imagined he was that cruel.

Suddenly I wasn't just afraid of having my butt kicked over that broken windshield. I was afraid for my life.

THE GUN

2 DAYS TO GO

I WENT TO SCHOOL EARLY Monday morning, just like Daniel had said, though I still had no idea what we were going to do.

The reserved spaces for the teachers were half-full and there were another two dozen cars at the far end of the lot near the football field. A handful of figures circled the track like ants, a potbellied figure with a whistle watching them. Even in Richie's day, Coach Gurdy always liked to practice first thing Monday morning.

I thought I'd beaten Daniel there, but as I crossed the front lawn he stepped out from behind a tree trunk, his face shadowed by a hooded gray sweatshirt. "You're late," he said.

"Sorry. It took longer than I—"

As the players stopped running, Daniel gestured frantically for me to get down. We ducked behind the front end of a Jeep Cherokee.

"They should go inside to shower in a minute or so," he said.

I was about to ask how he knew that when I heard the faint sound of a whistle. Sure enough, about thirty seconds later, I heard what sounded like a herd of elephants. I rose just enough to see P.J. laughing as he followed Schlong Schlom into one of the school's side doors.

My heart raced as Daniel reached into his bag and pulled out two things: a hammer with a taped-up handle and a crowbar with slight nicks in its metal surface.

"Choose your weapon," Daniel said.

"First you've got to tell me what we're doing."

Daniel surveyed the football field, where the churned up grass was still. Then he turned to the school, its brick walls desolate and lonely against the gray sky. Drops of rain began to patter down and tickle my ears and neck.

"I'll show you," he said, handing me the hammer. He strode across the parking lot, cocking the crowbar behind his ear, and marched up to P.J.'s Taurus. The new windshield was spread out before him as the metal whizzed past his ear. The crowbar struck the glass with a sound like a beer bottle being run over, the windshield spiderwebbing with cracks. I stared at it, stunned.

"Go ahead, we haven't got much time," he said.

I hesitated at first, not because this was wrong, but because I remembered what P.J. had done to that old woman's dog: tying it up, leaving it to die.

I realized there would be no justice for that dog or for me either unless I took it myself.

I went around to the driver's side and reared the hammer back, swinging it like a tennis racquet, aiming for the same place on the windshield where Daniel had struck. The window made a louder pop than I expected and a chunk of glass the size of my fist crumpled in on the dashboard. Rain slapped down in stronger waves and my hair dripped into my face, mixing with the sweat and burning my eyes like acid.

Yeah, this is even-steven baby, that's the way we play around here.

"Keep going," Daniel said.

I took another swing, smashing another star pattern in the center of the windshield. As I whacked the glass a couple more times, another chunk fell through, reminding me of Don't Break the Ice, a game Richie and I used to play when I was little. It had a tray of plastic cubes in a frame and a tiny toy hammer, the object being to tap

out single cubes without collapsing the entire sheet. This was the opposite, but it gave me the same sense of fun.

*You want to dick us around, this is what you're going to get, a
little payback.*

Daniel circled around to the side of the car, working on the passenger windows, and I crawled onto the trunk, taking a few good
whacks at the back window. After three good smashes, I almost
knocked it clear out of the frame. Daniel kept looking around to make
sure no one saw us, but I didn't care. I was swinging and bashing and
fighting the urge to let out a scream that would've carried clear to the
Hudson River.

I almost didn't hear Daniel bark, "Someone's coming."

The school's front doors were closed and the windows blank, rain
scratching against them. Then, whipping around to the road, I saw
Ross shuffle up the front path, adjusting the hood of his Wind-
breaker. Daniel had already ducked out of sight. I shoved the hammer
under my coat. At this distance Ross might not know what it was, but
he'd surely recognize me.

Shit, shit, get down, he'll see us.

I slid off the trunk and dropped down behind the Taurus as Ross
went into school.

"Come on," Daniel said. "We gotta go."

"Where?" I asked.

"Back toward my place."

"But we're—"

"—not supposed to be here yet," Daniel snapped. "It's got to
look like we showed up at our usual time."

"But what about Ross? He *saw* me." There was real panic in
my voice.

"Nothing we can do about that now. Come on."

127

But he stayed there for a moment, crouched by the back tire, and dug out the pocketknife he'd used on Richie's door lock. He jabbed the narrow blade between the rubber treads, unleashing a slow hiss, and smiled.

When he stood, slipping the knife in his pocket, I followed. He shoved the hammer and the crowbar into his backpack and we sloshed across the grass to the front gates.

I followed Daniel into town. He told me to wait behind a Dumpster in the alley while he went around to Schwamlein's Pharmacy. "What for?" I asked, but he said he'd be right back. When he returned, the rain had let up a little. Daniel had bought paper towels for us to dry off with. They kept tearing as I worked them over my head and face and finally the drizzle stopped. I felt refreshed.

"What do we do now?" I asked.

"Just go to school like nothing happened. If anyone wants to know, you came by my place early and we studied for English class. My parents left at seven, so nobody'll suspect anything." He shook his head like a dog who'd just come in out of the rain. "There's one more thing though."

"What's that?"

He held open the top of the Dumpster and tossed in the tools we'd used on P.J.'s car.

"There," he said. "No one can prove we did a thing."

When Daniel and I got back to school, a group of students had gathered around the ruined car. P.J. stood at the center, waving his arms, a tiny figure beneath the vast gray sky. He looked like he was recounting his football heroics, except that his face was beet red and the veins stood out on his neck. Turning away, I almost smiled, but the humor left me when I spotted Koryn on the front steps. She wore a brown sweater over baggy pants, an outfit that was more guy than girl, but she looked completely feminine. There was something blue in her brown hair, maybe a ribbon, but before I could tell what it was she slid through the front door.

A minute later I followed Daniel inside, wiping the last of the rain from my face. The adrenaline high of smashing the windows had begun to leave me, replaced by fear. Ross might have told someone what we'd done by now.

Daniel and I marched up to the third floor, our shoes squeaking on the staircase, and he led the way to room 339. I was about to follow when I nearly walked into someone. "Koryn," I said, thinking how this was just like the first day we worked together. But quickly I realized how different it was.

Daniel looked at her and then at me. I stood there, mouth open, and he shook his head and went into English class alone.

"Travis." Koryn said my name with more care than usual, making it sound almost foreign. She led me away from the door, past a row of lockers.

"I know I made a big mess at the mall but I just . . . I thought you liked me," I said.

Lee Kartinski walked toward 339, glancing back at us suspiciously.

"Of course I like you," Koryn said. There were scuff marks on the front of her right shoe, as if she'd kicked something. "I wouldn't have gone if I didn't. But maybe we just . . . it was kind of a misunderstanding."

"So you're with somebody."

"No, it's not that. I just . . . I don't really want to be with *anyone* right now." She half turned then, and I realized that the blue thing I'd noticed wasn't in her hair, it *was* her hair. She'd changed the color of the dyed braid from green to blue.

"But we're still friends, right?" The tentative sound of my voice caught me as sharply as a jab in the ribs.

"Sure, sure we are." I'd always felt Koryn was honest with me, but for once I couldn't tell if she meant what she said.

She started to walk away and then I surprised myself by saying, "I'm sorry."

Don't you go apologizing to her. That makes you as big a loser as she is.

Koryn nodded and walked away, her new blue braid swaying with the movement of her hips, and then it happened. As she was going into 339, Jordan appeared behind her. He said her name and she smiled. It was spontaneous, something she couldn't have planned, and in that moment she looked not just beautiful but angelic. Her face glowed, her eyes sparkled, her blue braid was offset by the sheen of her brown hair. I thought of all the images I'd drawn of her, where the nose or mouth or hair was always off, and the more I tried to fix it, the further I got from her essence. But this was what I'd been trying to capture all along.

Cheap slut.

There's nothing going on with them, I told myself, as Koryn and Jordan disappeared inside. He had a girlfriend already, and besides, she had just told me that she wasn't looking to get involved.

Not involved with us, anyway. The hell with her. The hell with him too. He stole your job, he stole your girl, why don't we steal a little something for ourselves?

I closed my eyes, the image of her frozen in my mind. When I opened them again, Moira walked toward me. Wobbled, really. She swung side to side with each step. She was wearing high heels, something she never did. I expected her to ignore me, but instead she said, "Hey Travis," putting a hand out against a row of lockers to steady herself. Pitching her voice a little lower, she asked, "Where's Daniel?"

"In class. Which is where I've got to go."

But I wondered: Had Ross told her how he'd seen me by P.J.'s smashed up car?

"This'll only take a second," Moira said. "I just wanted to say that I know you didn't take Ross's GameBox. And I'm sorry for blaming you."

"You are?"

"Because I know that Daniel *did* take it."

"No, he didn't. That's exactly—"

"Shut up and listen, all right?" She furrowed her brow and cocked a hand on her hip. "Daniel took the GameBox, but that's not all . . . Travis, I'm telling you this because you're my friend: you've got to watch out for him."

"You're not making any sense, Moira."

"I saw Daniel on Friday, on the way to the bus. I ignored him, but he came up to me and asked me how I'd like . . . if I wanted to have sex with him. I said no, and he said maybe you guys would both do it to me, together."

"Oh come on," I said, laughing. I knew Moira as well as anyone, and it was obvious that she was trying to create a wedge between me and Daniel.

"That's not all. He . . . he went, 'I know exactly what you like too. Travis told me all about you and him.' And I said that we never did anything, but then I thought about that time . . ." She made her voice real low, so that I could barely hear her. ". . . in the basement. And when I looked in his eyes, he knew, Travis. He knew about that."

"I didn't tell him."

"Then who did?"

"Ross maybe."

"Ross doesn't know," Moira hissed.

"Stop blaming me for everything, you dumb bitch," I said.

131

Moira looked up, her lips parted in surprise.

"You're so goddamn transparent. You've probably been preparing this little speech of yours all night. Then you come in here acting like you're my friend, and wearing those high-heeled shoes to seem like more of a grown-up, and it's all just bullshit."

"Unbelievable," she said.

"What's unbelievable?" Ross asked, coming up behind her.

I didn't care about Moira anymore. The question was this: how much had Ross seen and who had he told? I tried to read his face, the way Moira said she'd read Daniel's. Ross looked anxious but only a little, and he'd never been much of an actor.

"It's nothing," Moira told her brother, taking a step away from us. But Ross didn't go with her.

"Hey Travis," he whispered, "where is it?"

"Where's what?" I asked.

"You know, my GameBox. I didn't tell anyone, like you said in the note, but . . ." He looked back at Moira, who nearly fell off her heels. "I better go," he said as she clawed at the wall and pulled herself upright. Ross caught up to her easily.

"What note?" I asked, but if he heard me he didn't answer. Moira kept walking and made it to the stairs without losing her balance again. The late bell rung as I turned away, shaking my head, more confused than before.

When I went into class, everyone was at attention, notebooks opened, eyes riveted to the empty board. Mrs. Saxon flipped the pages of *Wuthering Heights*, oblivious to the door closing behind me. I felt all the heads in the room turn as one, marking me with their stares, but there was one person who didn't look. Koryn.

P.J.'s desk was empty. He was probably still outside, fuming about his windows. I slumped into my seat and Daniel looked at me, his eyes full of questions, but I shook my head and mouthed the word "later." While Mrs. Saxon continued her lecture, I got out my sketch pad, which was about a third full by now, and pictured Koryn as she'd looked in the hallway a few minutes ago. But just as I began to move the pencil across the page, there was a knock at the door.

Mrs. Burrows, Principal McCarthy's secretary, stepped into the room, tugging at the hem of her tweed jacket. "Excuse me, I hate to interrupt, but I'm looking for . . . Daniel Pulver and Travis Ellroy."

My heart stopped and when it started again it was going twice as fast.

"Well, go ahead, boys," Mrs. Saxon said, as if she wasn't sorry to see us go.

Daniel was already on his way to the front when I stood. But Mrs. Burrows said, "Perhaps you'd better bring your belongings with you." I'd already known that this was going to be bad, but that's when I realized just how bad.

"Where are we going?" Daniel asked as we all moved into the hall.

"Principal McCarthy's office."

"What for?"

"It's not my place to say." But her bow-shaped lips looked as though they would burst if she didn't tell someone.

Daniel snorted. "Well, I hope Principal McCarthy has a good reason for making us miss English."

Mrs. Burrows turned a corner without breaking stride. "Oh, it's not Principal McCarthy who wants to speak with you," she said, barely able to keep the smile off her face. "Sheriff Riley is borrowing his office."

New York State Police
interview with Sheriff Eugene Riley

DET. UPSHAW: Sheriff, when you questioned Travis about vandalizing your son's car, what kind of evidence did you have?

SHERIFF RILEY: Look, *Detective*, I really don't appreciate you coming in here like this, stirring up everyone with all these questions.

DET. UPSHAW: I apologize, but I have a job to do. And if I or any of my colleagues have interfered with—

SHERIFF RILEY: You know goddamn well you've done nothing but interfere since this whole thing happened. And you don't give a screaming shit about any of us.

DET. UPSHAW: (PAUSE) I'm very sorry, Sheriff, more than you can know. I'm a father myself. But I'd like you to answer the question—after your son's car was vandalized, what led you to—

SHERIFF RILEY: Look, I don't want your bullshit sympathy or your questions. In fact, I'm only going to tell you this one more time, and here it is: Travis Ellroy was jealous of my boy 'cause he played football and he had lots of girls around and that's not all. Travis was a screwed-up kid. His parents tried to do the right thing with him, but he wouldn't listen. Sometimes that's the way it is. Some kids are broken, and they just can't be fixed.

THE PRINCIPAL'S OFFICE WASN'T MEANT
for a man as big as Sheriff Riley. All six feet two inches and three
hundred pounds of him had squeezed into a small chair. With his gut
spilling out over the arms and his meaty hands clenched on the blot-
ter, he made the desk look like a toy. Principal McCarthy stood in the
corner, crossing his arms over his chest.

"Thank you for coming to see me, boys," Sheriff Riley said, as
if we'd had a choice. He looked at Daniel. "You must be Mr.
Pulver."

"I am."

Sheriff Riley gave me a sideways look. "Mr. Ellroy and I are
old friends."

He seemed to be waiting, so I said, "Yes, sir."

The last time I'd been questioned by the sheriff, I'd been so
wound up I thought I would bounce off the walls. This time, however,
I felt like a block of ice.

Asshole sheriff, we can take him.

"The sheriff and I would like to know where you two were between eight and eight-thirty this morning," Principal McCarthy
said.

Sheriff Riley looked annoyed at the question, but then he turned
to me for an answer.

"We were at Daniel's house," I said.

"Comparing notes for English class," Daniel chimed in.

"I didn't ask you, Mr. Pulver."

You didn't ask anyone, you fat pig.

"Daniel invited me to come over early, on the way to school," I said. "I got there a little after eight."

"If I talk to your parents, will they confirm your story, Mr. Ellroy?"

"Well, I . . . I said I was going to school . . . they don't know I was going to Daniel's."

"I see. And you, Mr. Pulver, will your parents confirm *your* story?"

"They'd already left for work. But I've got some of the notes we made if you want to see . . ."

"No, thank you, I don't."

Daniel shrugged. "You still haven't told us what this is all about."

Principal McCarthy moved up beside the sheriff. "Boys," he said, "we already know you smashed up P.J. Riley's windows and flattened his tire, so just be honest. There was a witness, and he says—"

Sheriff Riley whipped his head around so fast I thought it would snap off his neck. "I'll ask you to let me handle this, *Principal* Mc-Carthy. After all, it's a *criminal* matter." Sheriff Riley looked at me to make sure that was sinking in. "By the way, he's right. We do have a witness who says he saw you attacking my son's car."

Stupid Ross, goddamn ass, ass-licking asshole.

"Who's the so-called witness?" Daniel asked.

"I'm not sure it matters," Sheriff Riley said.

"It does to us. Because we didn't do anything."

"Well, he didn't leave his name," Sheriff Riley said. "But he told my dispatcher that he'd seen two boys smashing the windows on a black Taurus, and one of them appeared to be Travis Ellroy. When we figure out who made that call, we'll question him and find out what else he knows. In the meantime, Mr. Ellroy, you still owe three hundred dollars for that windshield."

"But he already paid the first one fifty," Daniel blurted, jumping out of his chair. "I saw him."

"Sit down." Sheriff Riley spoke quietly, but his words were more menacing than if he'd shouted them. "You haven't given me a dime, Mr. Ellroy."

We'll give you something, won't we, Trav-oh?

"I gave it to P.J.," I said. "Last week."

Sheriff Riley jerked his head back. There was something I couldn't read in his eyes, a different kind of anger than I'd seen before. "You were supposed to give it to me," he said. Had he told me that? I thought back to the conversation with him and my parents in the police station, but it was hazy.

Sheriff Riley stood. "Would you mind waiting outside, Mr. Pulver?"

Daniel shrugged, as if it didn't matter, but I saw the suspicion in his eyes: what was Sheriff Riley up to? Or was he afraid that I'd say something I shouldn't?

As Daniel turned the doorknob, Sheriff Riley nodded at Principal McCarthy. "You too, if you don't mind."

"But this is my office, Sheriff."

"And this is *my* investigation, Lyle. Perhaps I didn't make that clear."

Principal McCarthy hesitated for a moment, then nodded and said, "I'll be outside." I swallowed a lump as the door closed behind him. Instead of sitting back down, Sheriff Riley leaned his butt against the desk.

The end of period bell clanged in the corner and I looked up at the wall clock. It was almost ten, two hours since we'd smashed the car windows, but it felt longer.

"You going somewhere?" Sheriff Riley asked.

"I'll be late for my next class."

He sighed and just like that, the soothing voice was gone. "This I'm-so-innocent shit won't wash with me, Mr. Ellroy. I know what you are."

And we know what you are, a fat cop with a steroid-packing retard for a son.

"I also know what you're capable of," he said. "You smashed up my boy's car, just like you threw those rocks, and God only knows what you'll try next." I was silent, and Sheriff Riley put a sausage-sized finger to his chin as though he'd just had an idea. "I could let you off a little easier if you cooperate. Just tell me what happened out there."

I was silent for almost a minute until Sheriff Riley lunged up from the desk. He leaned over me, pushing his face into mine.

"You dumb kid, you're not going to walk away this time. You'll get what's coming to you, every last little bit of it, and you'll gobble it up like caviar."

Gobble this, you prick.

"It wasn't me," I said in a small voice, and it was true. Whoever had been in the parking lot, whoever had enjoyed the sound of cracking glass and the slash of rain, was not the person who now shriveled under Sheriff Riley's stare.

"Go ahead, get out of here," he said. "I don't want you to be late for class. But you'll be hearing from me, Travis. Soon."

And you'll be hearing from us.

As I walked out, I realized two things: the first was that the sheriff had called me Travis. The second was that his parting words sounded like one of P.J.'s threats, only with the force of law behind them.

At lunch I told Daniel everything that happened after he left the principal's office. He listened intently, not saying a word, but he didn't seem concerned. That made me feel better, but only a little.

Picking at my cold french fries, I looked over at the football players' table. Jordan, Amy, and Taffy were all sort of quiet. P.J. still wasn't with them. Was he so upset about his car that he'd gone home, or was he at the sheriff's office? I imagined him huddled with his father, the two of them making plans to get revenge on me.

Turning back to my lunch, I saw Ross and Moira at our old table. I tried to catch Ross's attention, but he wouldn't meet my gaze.

That stupid crybaby, that rat, we've got to make him pay.

I wondered again if he'd told Moira, and if she in turn had told him how I'd treated her earlier. I felt almost bad about that, but as soon as I remembered how she'd treated me, I knew I'd done the right thing. She was a manipulative bitch, and she'd gotten exactly what she deserved. But that still didn't solve the problem I had with P.J. and his father.

"What do you think the sheriff's going to do?" I asked.

"Nothing," Daniel said. "He hasn't got shit or else he wouldn't be pushing us so hard. He might use our parents to try to convince us to come crawling to him, but that's about it."

"But the witness—"

"Doesn't matter." Daniel chewed a piece of hard corn bread as he looked at Ross. "If he wanted everyone to know who he was, he would've given the police his name. He's too chickenshit. He won't bother us."

I hoped Daniel was right.

"There's only one thing we can do now," Daniel said.

I looked up at him.

"The list."

He held out a red pen and I dug into my backpack and pulled out the list, smoothed it out on the table. By now it was as soft as cotton and worn at the edges. I was careful not to tear it, as though it were old parchment, and glanced at some of the names that ran down the page—P.J. Riley, Gus Benedict, Moira Lansbury.

I wrote Ross's name first, since I was sure he was the one who'd gotten us in trouble at school. But it didn't feel as good as I expected. Then I put down Principal McCarthy and Sheriff Riley, for the way they'd treated us that morning. The memory and the act of writing got my adrenaline going, and I felt a natural high.

"There's still one person you forgot." Daniel held up his spork for emphasis, a piece of meat speared on it. "That conniving, back-stabbing little slut. Koryn."

He's right, that pissdyke, she's top of the list.

"She treated you like crap. She used you. I hate her guts, and I barely even know her. You must hate her twice as much. You probably wish you could take that hammer and beat the crap out of her."

But did I? Maybe the night after she left me in the parking lot, or even the next day. But now I was remembering all the reasons I'd wanted to go out with her in the first place, and I was hoping maybe we could patch things up.

Patch things up with that bitch? You're dreaming, Trav-oh.

As I started to write Koryn's name, the pen was stopped up. I made a small circle on the edge of the paper. The red ink finally came, but then I hesitated, thinking about Koryn in the hallway and the new sketch I'd been about to start in English class. And that's when it came to me. When Koryn saw the new sketch, drawn exactly as I wanted, when she understood how much I liked her, *really* liked her, and how much I wanted her to really like me, she would be so moved that she'd have to forgive me. Soon we'd be friends again, and maybe even more.

And best of all, she'd smile at me the way she smiled at Jordan. "I'll just do it later," I said, rubbing at the red spot on the list.

"You better," Daniel said. "And I hope you're not thinking about trying to make up with her. Because a girl like Koryn, she screws you once and she'll keep on screwing you. I'm serious, Travis."

He's right. We've got to do something, we've got to—

"I know," I said, looking at the list.

Ever since I kissed Koryn the other night, I've been feeling guilty. It doesn't mean anything, right? I keep telling myself: She was upset. It was late. We were tired. It just happened.

But I don't believe that.

I tried to be extra nice to Amy this morning. Opened her door when she got to my car. Gave her an extra long kiss.

"Well," she said, "what's gotten into you?"

"Just glad to see you," I said.

First thing I saw at school was P.J., standing over his car. Screaming. I didn't get it at first. But all the windows were broken.

"What's going on?" Amy asked.

"Hell if I know."

We went over. Amy didn't get too close. P.J. must've been scaring her.

I looked at him. Trying to tell him to cool it with my eyes. "I'm sorry. Your brand new windshield and everything."

"I'm going to kill those punks," he said. Kept saying it.

"Kill who?"

"Travis and his little friend Daniel."

"Do you know for sure it was them?"

"Oh, I know," he said. His voice told me there was no use arguing.

P.J. had called his father, who showed up a couple minutes later. Suddenly P.J. was calm. Or maybe he was scared too. His dad has that effect on people.

"They're really going to get it, aren't they?" Amy said.

"Who?"

"Travis and Daniel."

"P.J.'ll calm down. At least I hope so."

I'd been thinking about Koryn. How I ought to tell her that it was nothing. What we did. And how I wanted to tell her the opposite. That it was everything.

I left Amy at class, kept going. On my way into English, I saw Koryn. "You dyed your braid," I said. It was the first thing I could think of.

"I do it every once in a while," she said, sounding cheerful. But her smile was sad.

We walked into class together. I still wanted to talk to her. Really talk. And I wanted to kiss her again too.

P.J. never showed up at English. Then Travis and Daniel got called out to the principal's. Were they really dumb enough to smash those windows?

I checked for P.J. after second period and again after third. No sign of him. I saw Koryn on my way to fourth-period Latin. She walked faster than I did. Like she was avoiding me.

I was getting worried about P.J., so I found Amy and borrowed her cell. You're not supposed to use phones in school. I went to the bathroom to dial. P.J. answered on the first ring.

"What's going on?" I asked. My voice echoed against the pipes.

"Those assholes," he said, and then he was real quiet. That scared me more than the look I'd seen in his eyes earlier.

"Didn't your dad take care of it?" I asked.

"Oh, yeah, he took care of it. Took care of me too."

"What're you talking about?"

"Those pissants told my dad about the money they gave me."

"So?" I asked, not getting it.

"So? So? So my dad gave me a bunch of money last week. Money to fix the windshield."

"Ah, P.J." Double-dipping? That was just stupid. But he didn't need an I-told-you-so. "Look, are you all right?"

"I'm fine. Just peachy."

"Don't do anything stupid," I said. But I wasn't sure he heard me. There was a dial tone in my ear.

P.J. WAS THE LAST PERSON I expected to see on my way to Coffee Time. I'd left Daniel in the front lobby after school because he said Principal McCarthy had arranged a three o'clock meeting with his parents. I didn't know why I wasn't being called in with my folks too, but I felt lucky to be able to put that off for a little while.

Don't you worry. They mess with us, we mess with them. That's the way it is from here on out.

On my way out of school, I stopped at my locker to drop off a couple of books and found that someone had slipped an envelope inside. Opening it, I saw a piece of paper with Moira's handwriting. She had written: MAYBE THIS'LL CHANGE YOUR MIND ABOUT DANIEL. On the other side was a printout of a newspaper article. I skimmed it quickly, but there weren't many details. A boy named Paul Feezer had been out in the woods near his house when he fell through a hole in a partially frozen lake and drowned.

I didn't see what this had to do with Daniel. But near the end was a quote from "Daniel Pulver, a friend and classmate of the deceased." It said, "Paul was a great guy and I'll always miss him." So what was the big deal? I thought. And then I looked at the picture that went with the article: This was the same boy I'd seen in the photo on Daniel's desk. Crumpling the article and tossing it away, I wondered why Daniel had never mentioned Paul.

I walked quickly, head down, breath coming out in tiny clouds. I thought about how close I was to fixing things with Koryn and that made me happy. I barely even felt the sidewalk beneath my feet when P.J.'s Taurus charged in front of me, plastic bags wagging over its open windows, engine screaming.

I started to run.

Stumbling down the sidewalk, I looked for an escape, but the glass storefronts penned me in like a hamster in a tube. I was about to bolt for the opposite side of the street when the Taurus slammed against the curb ahead of me. Whirling, I ran back the way I'd come, even as I heard P.J. shout, "Get back here, you little bitch."

I resisted the urge to look back, feeling the burn in my calves and ankles, hearing P.J.'s footsteps on the pavement. Despite the icy breeze, sweat squeezed out of my pores. My legs pumped like cylinders, my breathing as ragged as an old dog's.

Stop running, you loser, stay and fight. We can take him, we'll give him a piece of—

"You shit!"

P.J. tackled me around the waist, bringing me down hard and fast. My chest smacked the ground, knocking the air out of my lungs, rattling my teeth.

"Did you think you were going to get away with this, you little monkeypisser?"

Piss on yourself, you good-for-nothing bastard. We're not going to take any more of your—

The sharp edge of an elbow jammed into my side, just below my ribs. Gasping for breath, I inhaled a scent that reminded me of metal shop.

"No, I—"

His fist knocked the words out of my lips and the thoughts out of my head. P.J. hit me again and I flopped back, half sitting and half lying on the ground. Then he started kicking me with his boots. He nailed me in the stomach, once, twice, three times. I thought of what he'd done to that poor dog and wondered if he would ever stop.

But he did, and that's when I finally got a good look at him. There was a bruise high on his face, just above his eyebrow, and a clump of dried blood under his lip, which was swollen. Someone passing by would have thought I'd done that, but I hadn't even gotten in a punch.

P.J. spit a gob of saliva at me.

"God, you're such a pussy."

He's right, get up, get up and get a piece of him.

But I didn't have the strength to stand, let alone go after him. My cheeks stung from the cold, my face hurt in too many places to count, and my stomach muscles ached so bad they felt like they'd burst. I wanted to die.

Go ahead, you little crybaby, cry a goddamn river.

But as P.J. revved the engine of his Taurus, I didn't shed a tear.

When I got home, the driveway was empty and the shades were drawn. I thought I was alone, and if I had been I might've finally broken down. But Daniel rose from the front steps, holding up a hand to block the sun. "I thought you'd be at work," he said as I moved along the shadows from a row of hedges. "But Jordan said you never showed."

"And you're supposed to be meeting your parents at school."

"My dad couldn't get out of work, so they canceled it," he said as I stepped out of the shadows. "What the hell happened to you?"

Ignoring him, I went carefully up the front steps, feeling the muscles in my calves cramp. My wrist ached as I turned the key and went across the living room. Daniel followed me. I shut myself in the bathroom and leaned back against the door.

"Shit," Daniel said, shouting to be heard. "I knew P.J. would be pissed, but I didn't think he'd ambush you."

I stared into the mirror behind the door, touching a green bruise beside my nose. My eyes were bloodshot and my skin was red from scraping the cement. "If we had just gotten the rest of the money somehow and left his car alone . . ." But I couldn't finish the thought. The blood in my head was pounding too hard for me to think clearly.

"If we had done all that, he still would've found a reason to beat your ass. This way, you earned it."

"*We* earned it," I said, whipping open the bathroom door. "Only I got shit for it and you didn't."

Daniel squinted at me, arms folded across his chest. I'd been hoping for an apology, but I saw immediately that it wasn't coming.

"What're we supposed to do?" he asked. "Just lie down like a couple of dumb dogs? He hates our guts, Travis, and he's going to do anything he can to punish us. If you just want to take it, fine, that's your business. But I'm not going to stand for it anymore. And I don't think you should either."

"So what're you saying?"

"It isn't over, Travis. Not by a long shot. P.J.'s going to keep on coming after you unless you do something about it."

"Like what?"

"I don't know yet. Let me think about it." He put a hand on my shoulder. "But I want you to know, I don't abandon my friends. Ever."

I studied his eyes and saw truth and anger, and I felt a little warm where his hand touched my shoulder. But there was still something bothering me. "What about Paul Feezer?" I asked.

"What about him?" Daniel stuck his hands in his pockets and half shrugged. "Did Moira tell you? Well, it's no secret. Paul was a guy I knew in Buffalo. He had a pretty horrible accident."

"It said in the article that he was your friend. I thought you stand by your friends."

"I do."

"Then how come you never mentioned Paul?"

"It's complicated, all right? We *were* friends, but by the time he died, we barely hung out anymore. We'd both been getting picked on by these kids at school, and I wanted him to stand up for himself. To show that we weren't pushovers. But he wouldn't. He let them roll right over him, and I guess I did too. Of course that's not in the article, and neither is this: he never would've gone out on that lake where he died. Never. It was really bright out there and when the sun was strong, he knew the ice could be pretty thin. If he was out on that lake, one of the school bullies must've chased him there."

"But that means—"

"Yeah. Whoever chased him basically killed him."

Daniel let that sink in for a moment and stepped away from the bathroom. I washed out my cuts and applied Band-Aids to my elbows, not sure what to say. I identified all too easily with Paul Feezer. I imagined myself getting chased out onto a patch of thin ice, plunging through.

When I left the bathroom, I expected to find Daniel in my room or in the kitchen. But he was at the door of Richie's old room, jabbing the tip of his pocketknife blade into the knob's keyhole.

"What're you doing?" I asked.

"I told you my secret. Now I want to see yours."

"Don't," I said, but my voice had no passion.

Hell yes, go in there, it's about goddamn time.

Daniel kept poking with the knife, producing little clicks. He won't be able to open it, I thought, just as I heard a click that was louder than the rest.

"Go ahead," Daniel said.

Go ahead, open it, open the door.

Helplessly, I thought of the last time I'd tried this. Being confronted by my father, feeling him slap me. Daniel knew about the rock-throwing incident but not what had led up to it. I reached for the knob and the door moved smoothly away from me.

Let's get in there, Trav-oh, and take what's ours.

The first thing I noticed was that Richie's room didn't look much different from when he'd died five years earlier. There was a Nirvana poster on the wall and a Pearl Jam one beside that, both held up by yellowed Scotch tape. A stack of CDs was piled on the boom box on the nightstand. A set of keys dangled off the desk as though Richie had just left them there.

I waited, half expecting to hear my father's voice, but there was no one to stop me this time. "Why'd you want to get in here so bad?" Daniel asked. "You looking for something?"

Instead of speaking, I searched. I started with the tall dresser, digging through Richie's outdated clothes, his musty smelling socks and T-shirts, even his *Playboys* buried in the bottom beneath his old practice jersey. My mother had been in here a hundred times, she must have, because every surface shone, yet she hadn't changed anything.

But that wasn't quite true. Before he died, Richie had packed his football trophies into a box and threw them in the closet. Now they were displayed where they had been all through junior high and high school, on the top shelf of his desk hutch, the gold plastic figures frozen in action poses. I couldn't read the inscriptions, but I knew them by heart—Most Improved Player, Most Valuable Player, State All Star. The same name was on every one of them. Richie Ellroy, Richie Ellroy, Richie—

"—Ellroy," Daniel said. Turning, I saw him holding Richie's copy of the school yearbook, which he'd pulled down from under the trophies. " 'One of the most dedicated and devoted students I've ever had. You will be missed, but never forgotten. Best wishes, Mrs. Saxon.' "

She would never write anything like that in my yearbook, I

thought as I prowled the room, rooting behind trophies and through desk drawers and under the bed. Finally I started on the closet. The first thing I saw was Richie's green and white Mongoose. He'd gotten the bike for Christmas the year he was twelve, and I'd always wanted one just like it. I touched the rubber grips on the handlebars and smiled, remembering the few times he'd let me take it out, how smoothly it rode, how fast it could go.

I returned to my search, flipping past Richie's old suit and the shirt and tie he'd worn to graduation. There was even his old football uniform, the blue jersey and white pants neatly pressed inside plastic.

"You should try it on," Daniel said over my shoulder.

"It won't fit. Richie was a lot bigger than me."

"Who cares?"

Do it, do it, do it.

I yanked the hanger off the rod and laid the uniform on the bed. Daniel turned his back to me as I pulled off my sneakers and pants. To my surprise, the football pants were just about the right length, and the jersey slid neatly over my head. It was too baggy, but I liked the coolness of it against my skin.

When Daniel turned back I saw a wild kind of glee in his eyes. "It's perfect. But where are the pads?"

As I dug through a bunch of old board games and baseball bats, I deliberately avoided looking at the mirror on the back of the closet door. I found the shoulder pads and the helmet way in back. Pulling them out, I saw that nestled inside the helmet was a small package wrapped in blue paper. Hands shaking, I set it on the desk.

"What?" Daniel asked.

"This is what I was looking for. My last birthday present for Richie. I never got to give it to him." I swallowed a huge lump. "He was dead before I had the chance."

I'd left the gift at Richie's door a few hours after I'd learned that he'd died and it was gone when I woke up that next morning. I knew deep down that one of my parents had hidden it away, but part of me had always believed that Richie's ghost had come for it, and brought it to the next life.

"What's inside?" Daniel asked.

"Open it," I said.

He tore the paper carefully, the way adults do, and then the kid in him took over and he ripped the rest away roughly. His fingers went around a long white box, finding the tucked in flap, even as the word "No" rose to my lips and fell away.

Inside the box was a trophy settled in a nest of crumpled tissue paper. The figure on top had a ridiculous pose, muscular arms crossed at the waist like a bodybuilder. This trophy was smaller than the ones on the shelf and the cheap gold paint had faded so that there was little shine to it. A plastic plaque on the base had WORLD'S GREATEST BROTHER, RICHIE ELLROY etched into it.

I felt a cold space in my stomach, thinking about the twenty-five dollars I'd spent on the trophy, a month's allowance. My parents had wanted me to get something less expensive, but I wouldn't let them talk me out of this. Now, though, I saw what my parents had seen all along, how pathetic and slight this trophy looked compared to the others.

I reached for it, desperate to put it away and lock the door and pretend I'd never been here. But Daniel held up the helmet and said, "We're not done yet."

I knew what he meant, but whatever joy I'd felt at first was gone. Still, I started to yank the helmet on. The foam casing pinched my ears, but when I tugged on the bottom of it, the plastic shell slid down neatly. I put the shoulder pads inside the jersey and Daniel helped adjust them until they sat just right.

Turning to the mirror inside the closet, I was struck by two things: the first was how much I looked like Richie. I imagined I was on the ten-yard line, dodging players who hurled themselves at me, and there was the goal line just ahead, P.J. and Jordan charging from either side.

But then I looked past the image of myself to Daniel's reflection, and noticed the second thing: his eyes were blank, as though he were in a coma, and his mouth hung straight across his face, the smile from earlier gone. It was as if the Daniel I knew was just a mask pulled on over this face, and the real Daniel was buried deep inside, in a place too dark and too deep for even me to reach.

When I turned from the mirror, his face looked normal again. I felt relief mixed with concern, but had no time to pursue either. There were footsteps in the kitchen.

Shit, shit, shit.

I tried to whip the helmet off, but it was too tight. I struggled with it even as my mother stepped into the doorway. She looked at me as though I had just stuck a knife in her heart and twisted. "Travis, what on earth are you . . ." She didn't know how to finish the thought, or couldn't bear to. "What's wrong with you, Travis?"

"Nothing. We just . . ." There was a lurch in my stomach, as though I'd just stepped off a roller coaster.

Go ahead, tell her. We just wanted to stop pussyfooting around Richie's corpse for a change.

"It wasn't Travis's fault," Daniel said, and for some reason I thought he was talking about Richie's suicide. "I was the one who made him come in here, I got the door open, I—"

"Get out of this house," she said, the anger starting to erupt. "Get the hell out *right now!*"

I thought she meant both of us, but when I started to move her eyes pinned me. Daniel looked down at the plastic trophy in his hand, then set it gently on the desk and started for the door. She moved aside to let him go, never looking away from me.

"Have you been in here before, Travis?"

"Obviously I've been in here."

"I mean since . . . you know what I mean, dammit."

"No."

"Well, you'd better not do it again. I swear to God . . . how could you do this to me? How dare you?" She shook her head. "You're sick, Travis. I'm taking you to see Dr. Hawke this time whether you like it or not. Maybe he can help you, because God knows I can't. I've tried to be a good mother, I've tried to help you, but nothing works. The principal called me, told me about what you did to P.J.'s car."

"Well, he's lying."

"Even if he is, look at everything else—you don't listen to me anymore, your grades are terrible, you get in fights at school . . ."

When she mentioned fights, I figured she was referring to my bruised face and the Band-Aids. But how did she know I hadn't just fallen off my bike or something?

My mother continued her tirade, her fingers gripped into fists. "I just don't understand you, Travis. What's wrong with you? Why can't you be more like Richie?"

Are we going to take that, Trav-oh? Are we going to take that bullshit?

"Well, Richie's dead," I said, feeling the anger simmer beneath my words. "Is that what you want? Another goddamn corpse around here?"

My mother gasped and covered her mouth, backing away into the kitchen. I heard her voice a moment later, and she sounded like she could barely get the words out. "Dr. Hawke, this is Eleanor Pulver . . . I, it's . . . please call me at home, I need . . . it's urgent."

When she hung up, she was almost hyperventilating. But I didn't care. I was about to go out there and really let her have it when I heard the front door open.

"Thank God you're here," my mother said.

"What's going on now?"

"He's out of control . . ." My mother must have realized I could hear her, and her voice faded to a whisper. I missed the next part of what they said, but then I moved to Richie's door and picked up the rest. ". . . need to talk to him. Right now, Thomas."

"What do you want me to say?"

"I don't know," my mother said. "Just find out what's wrong with him. I mean, two days before Richie's birthday and he pulls a stunt like this."

"I'll tell you what's wrong. He needs some goddamn discipline. He doesn't respect anyone or anything, that little ingrate, and—"

Oh, we'll give you some respect, give you all the respect you can handle.

The phone rang then and my mother answered breathlessly. "Oh, Dr. Hawke, thank you. Well, I should . . . let me get some privacy, all right?"

As my mother raced past the doorway, cordless phone pinched between her ear and shoulder, I heard my father from the kitchen. "I don't care what that quack has to say, Eleanor. This is a family matter, and I'll take care of it. I mean it."

But she didn't respond, just slammed the bedroom door behind her. From the kitchen I heard the refrigerator opening and a bottle being popped open. Then silence.

I stripped off the football uniform and put my own clothes on, feeling somehow smaller. Then I shoved the trophy and the paper into the helmet and flung it into the closet, getting a last look at Richie's bike. I wished I could take it out for a ride.

I waited for my father to come for me but he didn't, so I retreated to my bedroom and turned up Kid Rock so loud I couldn't hear anything. I continued waiting for one of my parents to barge in, but they didn't. I stayed there for what felt like hours but might have been minutes, every sound drowned out by the music, staring at the ceiling.

The music was so deafening I didn't even know my father was at the door until I rolled over on my side. "There's someone here for you," he said, turning the volume down.

It was Gus. He wore blue jeans and a checkered shirt instead of his Coffee Time uniform. The regular clothes made him look small.

"Hello, Travis," he said.

"What do you want?" I asked.

"You missed another shift, and as I was telling your mother, this was your last chance." Gus frowned, and I realized how I must have looked to him with my Band-Aids and bruised skin. "You all right?"

"I'm fine. I don't want your goddamn job, anyway."

My mother put a hand over her mouth, as if the words had left her lips, not mine.

Gus looked at her and shrugged, as though this was typical of what he'd had to put up with from me. "I'm sorry, Travis, but I'll need your apron."

Oh yeah, how about we piss on it and see how much you want it then, you turd, you shit, you fool.

Bolting for my bedroom, I dug into my backpack and grabbed the balled-up apron. On my way back to the living room, I heard my father say, "That's not what he told us at all. Well, I can't say I'm surprised but . . ."

"I'm sorry I had to be the one to tell you this—" Gus began.

He stopped talking as soon as I appeared. My parents stood on either side of him, both staring into space.

My father turned, his face shadowed with a look of raw anger.

My mother was pale, a splotch of mascara running down one cheek. I realized what had just happened—Gus had told them that I'd never been promoted, that it was all a lie. I felt a rage so hot and red that I very nearly wrapped my hands around his throat and squeezed.

Show that prickless wonder what we're all about. Destroy him. Destroy them. Destroy, destroy, destroy.

"You prickless wonder, you're nothing, and I wouldn't work for you if it was the last job in the world!" I said.

"Travis!" my mother said as I hurled the apron across the room and tore back through the kitchen.

"Get over here right now!" my father cried, but I didn't stop to listen, just locked myself in my room. I sat and fumed and waited and plotted, thinking of all the things I could do to them. I turned up my music again, so loud my ears almost hurt, then looked at the sketch pad on my desk.

There was still one thing I could make right. Koryn. If I finished the drawing, if I could show her the way she looked in my eyes, she would know that we were meant to be together. Out of everyone, she would understand. Again I thought of the way she'd looked in the hall. The brightness of her smile, the creamy curves of her skin framed by flowing hair, the now-blue braid running down her back. For once I took my time with the details, laboring over each line, comparing the sketch again and again with my mental photograph.

Soon she looked at me from the pad, her hair hanging beside soft features, her eyes so bright that her smile felt real. This was just a fraction of what was in my head, but it was definitely the best work I'd ever done.

Smiling, I slid the sketch pad into my backpack and began to count down the hours until I had to go back to school.

New York State Police
interview with Ross Lansbury

DET. UPSHAW: Could you describe Travis's behavior those
last couple of days?

ROSS: He just ... he was really weird. You could barely talk
to him and if you tried you couldn't get a straight
answer out of him. And he was so angry.

DET. UPSHAW: What was Daniel's behavior like?

ROSS: Well, Daniel was Daniel. He was a little weird from
the beginning, but Travis just never saw it. The more time
they spent together, the less Travis seemed to get it, you
know? And the way Travis was acting, he just got worse
and worse.

DET. UPSHAW: Worse how? Did you know what he was going
to do?

ROSS: Oh no, I had no idea. But then again, after what he did
to me ... I just couldn't believe this was the same person
I'd grown up with. And all those things he did with
Daniel, it was almost like a bunch of dominoes. After you
knock the first one over, you can't stop them. They all
fall down.

24 HOURS TO GO

I DIDN'T SEE MY PARENTS again until breakfast. I'd skipped dinner the night before, so I was starving. I had two big bowls of cereal while my father drained his coffee cup, not saying a word. My mother only spoke to ask if I could pass the milk.

When my father had gone, my mother said, "I made an appointment with Dr. Hawke for this afternoon. For the three of us."

Sounds awful cozy, doesn't it, Trav-oh? Only we're not going.

"I'm not going," I said.

"Well, I'm not asking."

"I bet Dad's not going either."

"Yes, he is. Because he knows that we need to start doing something about . . . about us."

But we never did.

I hurried off to school, feeling physically tired but intensely alert, ready to give my gift to Koryn. I waited for her on the front steps, the cement cold beneath my jeans. My face still hurt from the beating P.J. had given me, but I'd already peeled off the Band-Aids.

I first saw her from a distance. She had her red jacket zipped halfway up, revealing a green sweater. I watched her, the page from the sketch pad rolled up like a diploma and clutched tightly in my hands.

A rush of students charged up the steps past me. I noticed them looking and whispering, their eyes drawn by the purple bruises and the scrapes, but I ignored them. Instead I tracked Koryn as she weaved between buses. "Koryn!" I called. "Over here!"

She started to turn, but then her head whipped in the other direction, toward the bushes. Jordan was a dozen feet away and closing the gap. He held a small green notebook against the leg of his baggy corduroys, one hand holding his crumpled football jacket, the one Amy usually wore. He spoke quickly and Koryn listened as he led her around the side of the school toward the football field. I followed.

They stopped at the corner of the building. Koryn was doing the talking, Jordan's fingers poking into the worn brick. As she finished, she squeezed his hand and then let go.

Told you she was a slut.

Finally he said something and she replied and he pulled her close, their lips connecting. A kiss. I backed away, nearly tripping over my own feet. I crushed the sketch between my hands, twisting, and jammed it into my backpack.

Shitheads deserve each other. Deserve to die die die.

My body trembled with rage as I went into school. I decided to storm up to English class, not sure what I was going to do when I got there. Then I saw Ross down the hall, entering the door marked BOYS.

I followed.

There was a kid at one of the urinals but it wasn't Ross. Only one of the stall doors was closed, so I knew he was in there. I ran water over my fingers and looked in the mirror, surprised at my bloodshot eyes. The kid at the urinal flushed and walked out. Ross and I were alone.

I waited, listening to the sound of water moving through the walls, but Ross stayed where he was. I pretended to leave, pulling the door open and letting it close. A few moments later there was the sound of grunting inside the stall.

He's shitting a brick. Shit on him. Shit, shit, shit.

I waited just inside the door, praying no one else would come in. They didn't. In a couple of minutes Ross was done and I heard the swish of the toilet and the snick of the lock opening. Ross had barely left the stall when I lunged at him, spinning him against the wall.

"You shit, how dare you rat me out, how dare you, you stupid lowlife shithead. . . ."

"Travis, what're you doing, what're you talking uh-b-b-bout—"

He was crying so hard he couldn't get the words out, and I had a sudden vision of Ross and I, camped out at his kitchen table during fifth-grade Christmas vacation. Moira was sick with pneumonia, so it was just us, and we spent the week playing board games: Life, Battleship, Careers. Sometimes if Ross won three or four games in a row, he'd make a couple of obvious blunders to lose the next one. I always pretended I'd earned those victories.

Then I thought about the sheriff, calling me a criminal and threatening to lock me up, and I brought my fist back behind my ear and swung. Ross moved at the last moment, but a couple of my knuckles connected with his nose. He fell back to the tile wall, blood swimming out between his fingers and spilling onto his Atari T-shirt.

"You shit, I thought you were my friend!" I roared.

"I was . . . I am . . . Travis, please, what's going on—"

"YOU TOLD ON ME!"

"No, no." Ross started to shake his head and then seemed to think better of it. "I saw someone by P.J.'s car but I didn't know it was you and I didn't know what was going on and I didn't say anything. I swear."

"Liar," I said, and plunged my fist into his stomach. He collapsed. "I hate liars," I added, wondering if the sheriff was the real liar. Maybe he'd been bluffing about having a call from an eyewitness.

No, no, no. Ross is a snitch, a lying snitch, and he deserves this. GIVE IT TO HIM.

I did give it to him, then I turned away so that I wouldn't have to look at his bloody face. "If you tell anyone about this, *snitch,* you're dead meat," I said, and hurried into the hall. There was blood on my knuckles but I wiped it off with a tissue. When I pushed into room 339, I was only half surprised to find that P.J. wasn't there again, and neither was Jordan.

Out there screwing your girl, screw him.

But no, Koryn was in the second row, hunched over her notebook. That didn't make any sense. I thought of the crumpled sketch of her in my backpack.

"Well, there you are," Mrs. Saxon said, whirling from the blackboard. But when she noticed what kind of shape I was in, her voice softened. "Are you all right, Mr. Ellroy?"

Without responding, I stumbled toward my desk and flopped into it, feeling the eyes of several people, including Missy Relling. She flipped a string of red hair behind her ear and whispered, "Forget to take your meds this morning?"

"Take this," I said, and showed her my middle finger. Daniel noticed the gesture and nodded.

Mrs. Saxon paced in front of the room, her baggy gray dress ballooning around stout legs. "Let's get back to Catherine, and the dilemma she faces as we approach the climax. . . ."

I pulled the list out of my backpack and set it on the corner of my desk. Then I unfolded the creased paper and dug out the red pen from Daniel. I traced a line down with my finger and wrote Jordan's name in big block letters, printing carefully. I added Koryn right underneath, taking my time with each letter—the hard angles of the *K*, *Y*, and *N*, the curves of the *O* and *R*. But writing her name didn't feel like enough, and when I looked at Daniel I knew he agreed. Go further, said the fire in his eyes. How? I wondered.

Slutgirl. SLUTGIRL. ALL GIRLS ARE SLUTS!!!!

I found my sketch pad and tore out a clean page, scribbling shapes and forms that gradually became a face. Koryn's. My first instinct was to slash at it until I tore through the paper, but then I had a better idea. I drew her hair, making it look chopped and raggedy. Then I drew one eye wide and gaping, while the other had an ice pick in it. With the red pen I drew blood rushing out of the hole and onto the floor.

I slid the page to Daniel. He stifled a laugh. Mrs. Saxon glanced over, eyes lingering, and turned back to the board. Daniel used his own pencil on the paper, shielding it so that I couldn't see.

When he was done, Daniel slid the drawing back to me. He'd added worms crawling into Koryn's eye. I nodded my approval, then studied the picture, wondering what to do to her next.

The body, I decided. I drew Koryn naked, exaggerating her breasts and hips so that she looked like something out of *Hustler*. Finally I added a long knife sticking out of her belly. Satisfied, I gave the sketch back to Daniel.

Mrs. Saxon prowled the room, finally stopping beside Jordan's empty desk and settling on Max Monroe. The shrill sound of her voice grated on my nerves even though I'd stopped listening to what she said. Daniel did some more work on the drawing. When he gave it back, I saw that he'd put worms around the knife and written on her chest in what was supposed to be blood: BITCH. The sketch was almost done, only it needed one final touch. But what?

As Mrs. Saxon walked along the windows, I started drawing again. I drew a troll-like creature, a beast with wrinkled skin and too-big eyes and lips that curdled in his three-eyed face. He had stumpy legs and a bulging chest, but there was one key feature missing. I made that as exaggerated as the rest of him, and I was almost done when I heard Missy blurt, "Oh my God!"

"What's going on?" Mrs. Saxon said, as I realized that I'd left the drawing exposed. Missy was staring right at it.

"What are you doing?" Mrs. Saxon asked, grabbing the sketch by a single edge.

"It's . . . I . . ."

She saw the sketch pad itself on the desk and picked that up too. Flipping through it, she took in all the drawings I'd been doing for the last couple of weeks: P.J. being eaten by aliens with razor teeth, Daniel and I firing guns in the woods with P.J.'s decapitated head as our target, Mrs. Saxon herself being approached at her desk by the Collector, and more.

"I want you out of my classroom right now." A sharp V had formed between her eyes. "Now, Mr. Ellroy."

I looked at Daniel, waiting for him to jump in, to find some way to save us, to save me.

There he goes ditching you again, the hell with him. He doesn't give a shit, no one does except ME ME ME.

Daniel looked down at his notebook, as if I weren't even there. I pleaded with my eyes, begging him to say something, anything.

"Get out of my classroom, Mr. Ellroy." Holding the sketch out like a dirty diaper, she pointed at the door. Missy Relling covered her mouth, but not enough to hide her smile.

I gathered up my notebook and backpack, listening to the snickers behind me. But I didn't care about Missy or anyone else, including Koryn. As I touched the doorknob, I looked at Daniel, but his eyes wouldn't meet mine.

Beth Kittinger drummed her fingers against a crystal vase on the corner of her desk, the green stems of flowers stabbing through the murky water. "As you know," she said, "Principal McCarthy wants to suspend you. What you did today, along with allegedly vandalizing P.J. Riley's car, has convinced him that you deserve severe punishment."

"I don't care," I said.

"Well, I do. Did you smash P.J.'s windows?"

"What does it matter? No one believes me, anyway."

"I'll believe you. If you tell me the truth."

I looked her right in the eyes. "No. It wasn't me."

She nodded, a fragile smile taking root. "I'm glad to hear that. While you're at it, maybe you'd like to tell me what happened to your face."

"I walked into a wall."

"Travis, really."

"Okay, a wall walked into me."

"If P.J. did that to you, you need to report him."

Sure, I thought, I'll report him and next time he'll break my teeth and my ribs and my skull. Next time I won't just walk away, I'll be carried off on a stretcher. Or worse, I'll end up like that dog in the woods.

Beth sighed. "I'm not going to pressure you to say anything you don't want to say. As for this drawing, I won't deny that it concerns me. But anger can be therapeutic, if it's expressed appropriately."

Express this, you stupid psychobabbling bitch.

"You're starting to work through your emotions, which is promising. But now you've got to go to the next step. You've got to learn how to handle your anger in constructive, socially acceptable ways. And I think I can help."

I folded my arms and stared out the window. The clouds were lifting and the silver bleachers shone in the light, painting a shadow on the grass. Someone sat there, hunched over, and at first I was sure it was Richie, the rifle cradled in his hands. I closed my eyes even as I heard the shot, as real and as loud as the end of period bell, but when I opened them I saw that it was Jordan, a notebook spread across his lap.

"I know tomorrow's Richie's birthday, and I'm sure it must be tough for you," Beth said. "It always is for me."

"It's been a long time," I said. Her office felt suddenly hot, the air as stale as a hospital's, and my ears were ringing the way they had on that first day of target practice.

"Yes, but time only dulls the pain . . . it doesn't erase it."

Erase this, you damn shrink wannabe.

"Can I at least get my sketch pad back?" I asked.

"No, Travis." She sighed. "I'm going to recommend to Principal McCarthy that he reconsider suspending you. But I'm also going to insist that you and I meet three times a week, during your lunch hour, to talk. And maybe we can get at the heart of your problems."

The problem is we hate you, now leave us alone.

"I don't have any problems."

"Everyone has problems, Travis. The point is to learn how to deal with them." She folded her hands and smiled broadly at me. "You could do so much, if you'd just give yourself the chance. You're a wonderful artist and you have a loving family and . . . just look at all the great things you've done . . . you've made a new friend at school, and you got that promotion at work, and you . . ."

Beth continued to talk, but I wasn't listening. I kept hearing what she'd already said: *you got that promotion you got that promotion you got that promotion.*

The only people I'd lied to about Coffee Time were my parents. And suddenly I thought again about what my mother had said about me getting into fights at school, and I realized that she *knew* about P.J. bullying me, even though I'd never told her. Someone else had. Someone else had told her plenty.

bitch liar bitchliar get that goddamn—

"You bitch," I said suddenly. "I get it now."

"Travis." Redness creeped up from the collar of Beth's turtleneck.

"My parents put you up to this. You don't care about me. They just wanted you to spy on me and report back to them. That's what you've been doing this whole time."

"No . . . absolutely not."

of course it is teach her a lesson a lesson she won't forget

The redness had spread from her neck to her cheeks. "I won't lie to you. Your mother . . . she asked to see me . . . she was concerned. But I told her that whatever happened between us was confidential, and it is. I apologize for not being honest about this but—"

"You bitch."

"—please, Travis, I really think that you and I can—"

"YOU BITCH!"

Standing, I pulled my backpack against me and turned to the cubicle's doorway. Suddenly the redness fled, leaving Beth's face bone white. "Travis!" she cried, but I was already in the hall, my sneakers squeaking on the tile.

In less than a minute I was gone.

Crazy day. I don't even know where to start. At the beginning, I guess.

Driving with Amy to school. We were almost there. And I just did it. Just said it. The words popped into my head. Like when I said "I love you." Only different.

I said, "Amy, I want to break up."

Amy didn't say anything back. Her mouth was open. Lipstick on her teeth. Hair blowing across her face. She didn't wipe it away.

"What did you just say?" she asked.

"Amy, I want to break up."

"Oh God, oh God . . ."

"Amy," I said. Not sure what else to add.

"It's because of Koryn, isn't it? Taffy told me you were screwing her, and I defended you. I *defended* you, Jordan."

"I haven't done anything with Koryn." Not a hundred percent true, but true enough. "It's not about her, anyway."

"Of course it is. You like her, don't you?"

"Sure, I like her. I like P.J. too, and Gus, and—"

"You really like her."

"No," I said, slowing down for a traffic light. "I really like you."

And that was when her eyes cut into me.

"I thought you loved me, Jordan."

She started crying then. Cried all the rest of the way to school. I felt like a real shit.

Soon as I parked, Amy jumped out and pulled off the football jacket. Threw it back at me. I grabbed it and went after her. She was too fast. She ducked inside of school. I was about to follow, but then I saw Koryn.

I called out. She came over. My heart was going a million miles an hour.

"Haven't seen you around," I said.

"Yeah."

"It's almost like you're avoiding me."

Meant for that to sound like a joke. It didn't.

So I said, "I think our next stop should be Cody, Wyoming. It's a little cheesy, but it's also got this great old west history. Saloons and hotels and this huge frontier museum, and you only have to drive a few miles out to see the mountains, the open plains. What do you think?"

"Jordan, I, I have to—"

"What? Have you got a better idea than that?" There was an edge in my voice. I took a deep breath. I wanted to tell her what I'd been feeling about her. About Amy. About everything. But I couldn't think of the words. So I said, "I'm sorry, Koryn."

"No, I'm sorry. For everything." Her voice was full of sadness. I looked at the football jacket crumpled in my hands and knew that I didn't have to tell her anything. She knew it already.

"Jordan," she said softly, and I leaned in to hear her better. "The thing of it is, I went out with this guy last summer, while I was working in the Bard College bookstore.

"He was a few years older than me, and he was taking summer classes. I really liked him. He knew poetry, philosophy, all kinds of things. He swore it would last, me and him, even when fall came and I had to come back here. But the week before classes started, I found him making out with this girl in the library. I just went home and cried for hours, and I never heard from him again."

"Well . . . that sucks. Are you still in love with him?"

"I . . . no. But look, the point is . . . I don't want to be the kind of girl who steals someone else's boyfriend."

"You're not, Koryn."

"Yes, I am."

I pulled her close. Kissed her. It felt so good, her lips on mine. My whole body hummed. She must've felt it too.

But I wasn't sure. She pulled away and her eyes were dark. Angry, but excited too.

"I'm sorry," I said. It was getting to be a habit. I looked across the grass. Saw Travis staring at us. She saw too.

"I've got to go to class, Jordan."

And that was it. She walked away.

I couldn't go into school after that. Sat here on the bleachers to write. It's cold, so I put Amy's jacket on. My jacket again now. I'm still sitting. Still writing. Still waiting. Don't know when I'll stop. Maybe never.

17 HOURS TO GO

I WOKE UP ON THE GROUND and stared at the sky, which was spread out like a huge reddish cloth. I sat up groggily, looking at my backpack, which I'd used as a pillow, and then around at the woods, trying to figure out how long I'd been there.

My day away from school hadn't been much fun. I couldn't go home, because I knew Beth or Principal McCarthy must have called my mother. On the other hand, if I wandered around town someone might see me and wonder why I was cutting class. That left me nowhere to go but the back streets, until I decided to head out into the woods behind Lasher Road. I found the spots where Daniel and I had shot target practice and I looked for where we'd seen the dead dog, searching the ground for blood or paw prints. There was nothing.

I was pissed at P.J. and Koryn and Jordan, at Sheriff Riley and Beth and my parents, but mostly at Daniel. At first the feeling surprised me. I tried to get rid of it, but the longer it stayed, the more right it felt. No one was going to whisper around school about what *he'd* done. It was me, just me, same as always.

we don't need him we don't need anyone

Around what must have been lunchtime, I slumped against a maple tree, and dozed off. I dreamed of a place far from Shadwell, where no one had to go to school and kids could live without their parents and every door was open to anyone who wanted to go in.

For a while I was happy.

As I woke up, however, the dream felt very far away, and with the sun falling from its cloud-mountain peak, the day's warmth began to vanish. Rubbing my arms, I wondered if my parents were still at home, waiting for me. The thought made me smile as I hauled my backpack over my shoulder.

Although I was still mad at Daniel, I couldn't think of anywhere to go but his house. Then I realized: what if one of my parents had gone there? Better to check out the situation first. I headed into town and found a pay phone in front of the IGA. I dialed Daniel's number, but no one picked up after four rings. I was about to hang up when a voice I didn't recognize came on the line.

"Hello?"

I was sure I must have the wrong number, but I said, "Is Daniel there?"

"Travis, what's going on?" Daniel's voice must have changed a little or maybe it was the way I heard it that was different. It had been him on the line all along. "Where are you?" he asked. "Where have you been?"

where do you think we've been we've been taking shit for you

"Your parents called a couple times," he said. "I told them I haven't seen you."

I didn't reply. There was a buzz of static across the line, smooth as a stone skipping water.

"You're pissed," he said finally.

I remained silent.

Daniel sighed. "I don't blame you."

"No, but everyone else does." I wanted to stop there, but I couldn't. "You helped me make that picture and then you let me hang for it, you bastard."

backstabbing bastard traitor

"This is all Koryn's fault," he said. "First she leads you on, then she starts screwing around with Jordan, and next thing you know she acts like *you're* the one who's got a problem. If it wasn't for her, you wouldn't be dealing with any of this shit. You can scream at me all you want, but she's the root of everything that's gone wrong."

He took a breath and went on. "I'm sorry I didn't say anything when you got caught with the drawing, but you're lucky I didn't get nailed too. At least this way it looks like an isolated incident. Some girl burned you, you got mad, end of story. If I was involved, somebody might start thinking, Hey, there's two of them, maybe they're crazy enough to do something."

"Crazy enough to do what?"

"Go after her," Daniel said. "She can't treat you like this."

"Well, she has."

"So are you going to do something about it or what?"

you know what to do and you don't need him to do it

I let out a long, shuddery breath. "I'm not sure," I said.

"Come on, you know how good it would feel to get a little revenge. I'm not talking about on paper, Travis. I mean in real life."

"How?" I asked, and my voice sounded very small.

"We've got our list," Daniel said. "Maybe it's time to use it."

I'd been waiting to hear those words, and dreading them at the same time. I wanted to hang up and find my parents and tell them everything, every single thing that had gone wrong since the night Richie died, but they wouldn't listen and if they did listen they wouldn't understand or do anything about it.

you and me trav-oh the hell with him the hell with everyone

"I'm going to come over," I said.

Daniel's voice got muffled and I heard, "All right, Mom, I'm coming." Quietly he said, "Travis, you can't. My grandmother died today. We're about to leave for the hospital so my mother can take care of all this funeral bullshit."

"Oh," I said.

There was static on the line again. It crackled as though there was distant thunder, but I saw no sign of rain in the sky.

forget him let's go already let's go go go

"It's time, Travis. Either you let everyone keep pushing you around or you make your stand. Right here, right now."

make a stand make a plan make everything even-steven

"You're going to help me, aren't you?" I asked.

"Of course I will. We're in this together, aren't we?"

"Are we?" I said, feeling a toxic wave of self-pity. "You can take care of yourself. You don't need me."

"That's not true," Daniel said, his voice stern. "Look, I've got to go. But we'll talk about this tomorrow. I've been working on a plan, and I think you're going to like it."

I wasn't sure what Daniel's plan involved, but whatever it was, "tomorrow" just wasn't soon enough. Didn't he understand that? I was sick with rage and struggling with a vile feeling I'd never known before. I walked so hard I thought I'd burn holes in my sneakers. I walked because I couldn't bear to stand still.

Finally I looked up and realized my feet had taken me to Coffee Time. I peered through the plate glass window and saw a single customer, a woman with a thick pile of black hair. Jordan was behind the counter.

I went in. The door pinged overhead, but Jordan didn't look up. "How can I help you today?" he said, and it was only when he reached "you" that he did a double take.

"Hi, Jordan."

The smell of croissants made me realize how hungry I was. I looked down at the glass case filled with them and saw my reflection. My hair was blown every which way, my shirt pulled out of my pants and stuck to my chest with sweat. Jordan, however, looked totally put together, with his starched shirt and clean brown apron. I imagined ripping the apron off, balling it up, and cramming it down his throat.

"Travis, you shouldn't be here," he said.

"Oh, I'm sorry. I thought this was a free country."

"Of course it is." He didn't smile, not exactly, but the corners of his lips crept up. "All right, what can I get for you?"

you can get the hell out of here you girl-stealing son of a bitch

His gaze burned like a heatlamp. Sweat beaded on my brow, but I didn't want to lift my hand to wipe it away. I stared at the menu board, as though I didn't know it by heart.

"I'd like a tall skim milk with vanilla syrup," I said.

He made no move to the drink bar. He knew as well as I did whose favorite drink that was.

"That is, unless you're out of milk or something," I said.

you tell him what we want and you make sure we get it

Finally, he rang the order up. I fished in my pocket for money. He set my change on the counter and glanced at the swinging door leading to the back. Was Koryn in there? I could almost see her coming out, me leaping over the counter, grabbing her and shoving her back against the coffee grinder, squeezing her throat until she turned white, then purple.

Jordan plunked a cup on the counter. As I watched him reach below the cappuccino maker for a jug of milk, I said, "No, syrup first. The way Koryn makes it."

He poured half an ounce of vanilla syrup, then splashed in milk and slapped on a lid.

let's go trav-oh show him what we're made of

"So how long have you been banging Koryn?" I asked, taking the cup.

"Travis, I've got to tell you, it's not—"

But before he could go on, the swinging door popped open, and Gus stepped out. He showed an instant of surprise but it vanished quickly.

"What are you doing here?" Gus asked.

"It's all right," Jordan said.

I lifted my cup and milk sloshed against the lid. "I'm just getting a drink."

"Looks like you've got it," Gus said. "So why don't you take off?"

I peeled off the lid and took a quick sip, surprised at how sweet it was. Looking at Gus, I thought about how he had humiliated me in front of my parents. There was no reason for him to come there and make a bad situation worse.

As I started to leave, I hurled my cup across the counter. Gus put his hands up as the liquid splashed on his face and rained into his hair. The cup itself dropped silently in front of him. Gus stepped on it as he bolted forward, plastic crunching as he reached across the counter and grabbed a handful of my shirt. My backpack slipped off my shoulder and crashed into the register.

I swung one fist wildly, but the backpack strap stopped my arm and my fingers barely grazed Gus's cheek.

"You stupid punk," Gus said, fists in front of him. Jordan grabbed at Gus's arm to restrain him but Gus brushed past him, circling the counter. The woman with the pile of dark hair looked up but continued to drink from her mug.

"Travis, get out of here," Jordan said.

"Actually, I'd rather you stick around," Gus said. "Because you've got three seconds before I call the cops."

I cocked my fist back as a threat, but Gus was bigger and stronger, and besides he had Jordan to back him up. The power I'd felt a moment ago disappeared, leaving me helpless. Whirling, I said, "Suck my tasty dick, you asswipes."

I pushed out into the dusk, the cold, the silence. The streetlights were on, though it wasn't quite dark yet. It didn't matter. Even in the black of night, I could have found my way, because for once in my useless life I knew exactly where I was going and exactly how to get there.

On my way into Shadwell Cemetery, I passed the graves of Civil War soldiers, their chipped granite slabs angling out of the dirt. As I went further back I saw the more recent stones, some with crosses or angels on top of gray marble.

My brother's grave had none of that. Block letters were carved in just like on his football trophies. There was Richie's name, the dates of his birth and death, and the legend: TAKEN TOO SOON. I'd never understood why my mother wanted it to say that, since it wasn't like he'd been hit by a bus. But she'd insisted, and my father hadn't had the heart or the guts to argue.

I'd never liked seeing my own last name on the grave, so I turned away, studying the rows of markers that stretched toward the horizon. Then I heard wheels chewing gravel behind me.

As I began to back away from the grave, I saw P.J.'s black Taurus, shiny new windows in all of its frames. At first I was paralyzed and then fear settled in my bowels and I ran.

don't run you wuss it's payback time give him what he's got coming

As the car groaned to a halt, a voice called, "Hey, wait!" but I didn't listen. I stopped when I heard the voice again, which was deeper and more booming than P.J.'s: "Travis, get back here!" It was Sheriff Riley.

He worked hard with each step toward me. A garage work order poked out of his pocket above his badge. "You'd never know I used to play football," he said, panting. I tried to imagine him as a star athlete, like P.J. or Richie. The image wouldn't come.

"What the hell do you want, Sheriff Riley?"

He looked surprised at the challenge. But it felt good to stand up to him because despite his badge he was just a fat man who couldn't run across a graveyard.

"You'd better show a little more respect than that," he said. "If you want to stay out of jail."

respect this you pig we're not going to jail

"I'm not going to jail," I said. "You haven't got any witness and you haven't got any case." Suddenly I sounded like the Collector, like someone who couldn't be pushed around.

"We don't have the witness yet," Sheriff Riley admitted. "But we *have* traced his call."

I tried not to look interested. "And why should I give a shit?"

"Well, maybe because the call was made at a pay phone in Schwamlein's Pharmacy at 8:20 A.M. yesterday. Clerk also says he saw your friend Daniel in there about a quarter after eight."

"So?" I asked.

"So nothing," he said. "Nothing at all. Except that maybe you're right. Maybe there *was* no witness."

Ross is the witness, I wanted to scream, and then I thought about what Ross had said: he hadn't known it was me who'd smashed the windows, and he hadn't told anyone about being there. But that didn't make any sense and neither did this. Sheriff Riley was lying, laying a trap for me, trying to confuse me.

you know who the liar is you know what's going on you're just too dense to admit that—

"This is bullshit," I said, spinning away.

"Come back here, I'm not finished talking to you." But Sheriff

Riley sounded as though he knew I wouldn't come back and that was okay. He knew what he'd planted in my head.

fathead shithead shit on you shit on everyone

I raced out of the cemetery, slowing as I reached Route 9, my steps as steady and even as a soldier's, my mind buzzing with questions. One way or another, it was time to get some answers.

New York State Police
interview with Daniel Pulver

DET. UPSHAW: Did you know what Travis's plan was
    that night?

DANIEL: No.

DET. UPSHAW: You didn't know he was going to your house?

DANIEL: No.

DET. UPSHAW: You had no idea what he was going to do next?

DANIEL: Of course not.

DET. UPSHAW: Do you know why he decided to take that
    course of action?

DANIEL: Not really. In some ways I was as surprised as
    anyone, but I guess I wasn't *that* surprised. The whole
    time I knew Travis, he was really ... angry. Always
    talking about hurting people, getting revenge.
    Everywhere he turned, he saw someone who'd done
    something bad to him, and I guess he thought the only
    way to make up for it was ... well, to do what he did. I
    feel awful though. I just wish there was something I
    could've done.

DET. UPSHAW: Did you know Travis was capable of
    doing this?

DANIEL: Not at all. If I'd even dreamed something like this
    would happen, I would've told someone. I would've stopped
    it. I would've done anything I could to make sure that no
    one got hurt.

WHEN I GOT TO DANIEL'S HOUSE, I was winded and red-faced from running. The pumpkin we'd stolen from the field out back sat on the top step. There was a spot of black rot showing under the stem, and it was probably even more rotten inside. Lights were on behind the living-room windows, but I wasn't sure if anyone was home. I rang the bell anyway. A few seconds later, a woman's voice called out: "Who is it?"

it doesn't matter just open the goddamn door

"It's Travis. Daniel's friend."

There was a pause before Madeline Pulver appeared. A pair of red-rimmed glasses hung on a chain around her neck. Even in her slippers, she stood half an inch taller than me.

"Danny's not here," she said.

and she's not supposed to be here either liar liar liar

"I'm sorry about your mother," I said.

"Excuse me?"

"Daniel's grandmother. The one who died."

She looked puzzled. "Daniel's grandmother died several years ago. Both his grandmothers, as a matter of fact."

told you so told you bullshit artist all bullshit

"Of course," I said, as though I'd been kidding in the first place.

"Anyway, Daniel's out with his father. Shopping. They're going to buy Danny some new video games. For his birthday."

"For his . . . birthday?" I practically coughed the word out.

She tilted her head sideways. "Didn't he tell you about his birthday? This weekend? We might even have a party for some of his friends."

we'll give him a little party won't we trav-oh

"Yes," I said, and squeezed my arms against my body so that my shoulders didn't shake. "He told me. I just . . . I guess I forgot."

"I see." Madeline Pulver sounded like she didn't see at all, and those red-rimmed glasses weren't going to make any difference. "When he gets back, I'll tell him you stopped by."

don't let her turn her back on us or she'll be—

"Sorry," I said. "That is, for bothering you."

"Oh, it's no bother."

I wondered what Daniel would do in this situation, but I already knew: he would find a way inside. So I scratched at the side of my face, doing my best to look embarrassed, and said, "The reason I came is, um, when I was over here the other day, I forgot some comic books."

"Go ahead up. I assume you know the way."

Her eyes flicked at the doormat, so I made a show of wiping my sneakers on it. I dropped my backpack there too and watched as she retreated through shadows to the kitchen.

The carpeted steps didn't make a sound as I went upstairs. I squinted along the dim hallway and stopped at Daniel's door. I knew that when I crossed the threshold there would be no turning back.

I went in. *The Matrix* poster loomed above me like an angry guardian and the dark windows reflected the room, making it look bigger than it really was. The space felt different than before, empty of something I only noticed because it was gone.

I didn't know what I was looking for, but I began digging through Daniel's desk, flipping through old copies of *Sports Illustrated* and *Maxim*. A wad of purple paper in the back of the drawer caught my eye. Reaching in again, I found a rubber-banded pile of purple stationery. Letters from Daniel's old girlfriend, Caitlin. Curious, I stuck a finger inside the rubber band and read part of a page.

Instead of the gooey, desperate pleas Daniel had told me about, the language was formal. *School is good. Everyone's studying for SATs, thinking about college, you must be too.* I pulled the rubber band off and read the rest of the letter, which made it clear this wasn't his girlfriend and never had been. There was more chatter about school and people I'd never heard of, but one passage caught my eye. *I can't believe it's been a year since Paul died. I still think about him sometimes and I'm sure you must too. . . .*

I crumpled the letter, black dots moving across my eyes, sweat beading up on my forehead. I started opening drawers at random, desperate to find more evidence of Daniel's lies. Nothing. Then in the bottom drawer, I discovered about twenty notebook pages. They all said the same thing: ROSS, MEET ME AT SCHOOL, 8:15, HAVE INFO ABOUT YOUR GAMEBOX, DON'T TELL ANYONE. They were all signed with my name and written in what might have been my hand-writing.

As I flipped through the stack of notes, I noticed that while the first ones were crude, the later ones were better, and finally even I couldn't tell that I hadn't written these.

I tried to put the pieces together, but I couldn't. What did Daniel want? Why had he pretended to be my friend if he wasn't? I was so furious I wanted to tear my own skin off, but also so desperate that I could see myself going downstairs and shaking Madeline Pulver until she told me the truth. But she wouldn't know it. Some secrets only Daniel could tell.

oh he's going to spill it all spill his guts all over the floor

Jumping on the bed, I grabbed the corner of *The Matrix* poster, the one that was just like mine. I tore the thick paper through Keanu's face, leaving half a mouth. I wanted to go around and shred every magazine and crack every DVD and gather everything in the middle of his carpet and light a big bonfire. Standing out in the front yard, I'd watch the house reduced to smoking rubble, but I wouldn't be satisfied unless Daniel was inside, roasting like a pig.

yeahhhhh cook that son of a bitch

I was about to jump off the bed when I noticed something on top of the bookshelf, beside a Buffalo Bills cap. It was a large book with a fake-leather cover and an *R* on the spine for *Reserved*. The school library's missing 1997 yearbook.

I flipped the stiff pages, spotting a picture of my brother with his arm cocked, fingers clutched around a football, and then I turned to the student "wills" section. There it was, RICHIE ELLROY'S LAST WILL AND TESTAMENT, and I read his final piece of advice, which I'd seen a million times but never quite this way: Don't do anything I wouldn't do.

My hands were shaking. Breathing deeply, I tucked the yearbook under my arm and made my way to the master bedroom.

The room smelled of incense and fresh laundry. My heart thundered in my chest and I felt the same sense of danger I'd had watching Daniel steal that comic book. I opened the top drawer of the nightstand. What excuse would I have if Madeline Pulver found me here?

who cares about her you know what to say you know what to do

I pulled the drawer a little wider, terrified that the Beretta wouldn't be there. But there was nothing to worry about. The Beretta's checkered handle curved right into my palm. I popped out the clip and filled it with slugs, making sure the safety was on before sliding the gun into my waistband. The metal was cool against my thigh and belly as I pulled my shirt over it.

I grabbed the half-full box of slugs and slipped it into my front pocket. Tucking the yearbook under my arm again, I padded out quietly. I realized I hadn't even taken what I'd supposedly come for: comics. I went back to Daniel's room and searched the pile of papers on his desk, finding a copy of *The Incredible Hulk*, the one he'd bought in Dungy's that night, plus a duplicate issue of September's *The Collector*, the one he'd stolen and given to me.

"Did you find what you were looking for?" Madeline Pulver asked, rubbing her eyes as I came down the stairs.

"Yes," I said, holding up the comics, the yearbook beneath them.

she wants to see what we've got why don't you show her

"Good, very good," she said. Then she smiled. "I just wanted to say thank you. I don't know how much Daniel has told you about where we used to live but . . . it doesn't matter. You've been a really good influence on him, and I'm grateful."

"He's been a good influence on me, too."

now how'd you like to go out with a bang you bitch

She reached out and patted my arm, as if we'd bonded somehow. "You'd better run along. I'm sure your parents don't want you out too late."

"No," I said, slipping the comics and the yearbook into my backpack, "I'm sure they don't."

In the night air, the gun felt like a block of ice pressed against me. I didn't mind. It kept me focused, which was good, because I wanted to make sure my aim was steady when I got home.

THE
COLLECTOR

14 HOURS TO GO

AS I CUT ACROSS THE LAWN to the road, I heard someone call, "You! Boy! Come here!" Turning, I didn't see anyone, and my hand went instinctively under my shirt for the Beretta. Then I saw the old woman next door at the bottom of her front steps, a long jacket blowing behind her like a cape.

forget her we got business to take care of let's go go go

I let my shirt fall back into place but I kept my hand close to the gun just in case. Mrs. Bonkers turned sideways to avoid the wind and her long coat dropped against her legs, suddenly deflated.

what are we doing here waste of time waste of ammo

"You're Daniel Pulver's friend," she said, her voice nearly swallowed by wind.

Was his friend, I thought, but didn't correct her.

"I have to warn you," she said. "You watch yourself with that boy. I tried to tell his parents what he's done, the sheriff too, but they won't listen. Nobody will."

"So?"

"So he killed my Alfie, my sweet little Alfie."

Hearing the name brought back the image: the broken dog in the bloody dirt, frayed rope around its neck. Of course Daniel had done it, I thought. I'd been a fool to think otherwise.

"Do you have a dog, young man?"

It was almost the same thing Taffy had asked, but this time I gave a different answer. "Yes. His name is Simms."

"Well, you be careful, you watch Simms like a hawk," she said, wagging a finger. "But it's not just your dog you've got to worry about. He'll do worse than you can imagine."

There was something about the rising pitch of her voice, the feverish look in her eyes. She was definitely one beer short of a six-pack, as Richie would have said.

"I know what kind of person Daniel is," I said.

"You've got to stop him. You've got to keep him from doing what he's going to do."

"I'm not sure I can."

"You have to. You're the only chance we've got."

chance this you crazy old bag

For a moment I saw the scene as if it were a panel in a comic book, me standing there by the edge of the broken path, her huddled against the cold. The colors were all green and black and red, the wind marked by white lines against a dark background. There was a bubble over her mouth that said, "You're the Collector. You're the only chance we've got."

And then a bubble from my mouth said, "I'll do what I can." In the next panel I was walking away, hands tucked in my pockets, and the woman was shouting at me, hands cupped to her mouth, screaming into the wind, as if she had something else to say, but I couldn't hear it. I was too far gone.

When I got home, it was quiet and the air smelled of burnt toast and spilled beer. There was a light on in the living room, but the front hall was dark. I flung my backpack on the kitchen floor and said, "I'm home."

"Thank God."

thank yourself you worthless bastard and leave us alone

My father put a hand to his forehead as he stepped out of the master bedroom, the cordless phone in one hand, a notepad in the other. His crumpled tie hung from his shirt and his belt drooped open.

"Where the hell have you been?" he asked.

"Yeah, well—"

"Oh, Travis," my mother said.

She burst out of the doorway, hair corkscrewed, eyes so red they matched her blotchy lipstick and her Shadwell High sweatshirt. The shirt used to be Richie's and she wouldn't get rid of it, even though all but a few of the letters had peeled off.

"You'd better have a good explanation for all this," my father demanded, and I almost laughed.

"For what, Dad? For throwing the rocks? For smashing the windows? For letting Richie blow his brains out? You tell me what you want an explanation for and I'll be glad to give it to you, you stupid shit."

there you go now you're talking you tell him you can't mess with us

"You can't talk to me like that." My father reached for his tie as though to straighten it. "I'm still your father, and I'll—"

"Leave him alone!" my mother shrieked. Turning to me, she sounded calm but not like herself at all. "Travis, I'm so sorry about everything. Beth told me . . . we only wanted to help. I never meant to hurt you, not at all, and I want to make things right. We're going to get through this. We'll see Dr. Hawke right now and he said that—"

"That shrink and you can both go to hell."

"Travis, please."

please yourself you dumb bitch

My mother flung herself at me, arms flying around my neck. I was afraid she'd feel the gun in my jeans but if she did, she had no idea what it was. The feel of her warm skin and hot tears against my neck made me want to puke.

do it trav-oh what're you waiting for show her what we got

"Leave me alone," I said, pushing her off.

"But Travis, I'm just trying to—"

"Go to hell!"

Her reply was soft, almost a whisper. "But Travis, we love you."

do it do it DO IT NOW

"Well, I hate you," I said, and pulled out the Beretta. My mother was too close for me to extend it fully, so I held it against my side. Seeing it, she gasped. My father's view of the gun was blocked by her, but he must have known from her reaction that something was horribly wrong.

"Don't!" she cried, but didn't move. She must have thought I was going to use the Beretta on myself.

fat chance bitch this one's for you

I jabbed the gun at her and she screamed, a sound so shrill I wanted to stick my fingers in my ears, and I thought about the cans on the log, the pumpkins, the dog with the rope around its bloody throat, and I screamed, "Bitch, this one's for you!" as I pulled the trigger.

The Beretta made more noise in the house than it had in the woods. My mother flopped over as though she'd tripped. Blood gurgled out of her stomach and she covered the wound the way she'd done for me when I was eight and had fallen off the back steps.

"Travis!" my father howled, dropping the phone and the notepad. I turned the gun on him and quickly pulled the trigger again, the slug whining as it took a bite out of the doorway behind him.

My mother rolled onto her belly and tried to crawl down the hall toward my father. But there was blood seeping out from under her and she couldn't get her arms and legs to move together. My father tried to lift her.

"Don't touch her."

"Travis, we need an ambulance, we need help. . . . " His eyes drifted toward the phone, which was at my mother's feet, between me and him. She was the only one of us that could've reached it, but her fingers curled against the floorboards, useless.

"I've got all the help I need," I said, and aimed the Beretta at my father's head.

He let my mother go and backed into the master bedroom, his eyes wide with terror. My mother made a "go" gesture with her chin, pleading with him to save himself, and I felt a fresh wave of heat inside me. I straddled my mother's back and sat like I used to on Richie when he gave me "horsie" rides. My father disappeared into the bedroom, shouting, "Travis, don't do this! It's not too late."

I brought the gun to my mother's head. To my surprise, my hand shook a little, especially when she spoke.

"Don't . . . please . . . I love . . ."

Her words were slurred, the syllables running together. From inside the bedroom, I heard rummaging and wondered what my father was doing. I stood up from my mother even as she croaked more broken phrases.

"Oh Guh . . . I love . . . don't hurt me, Richie . . . please don't . . ."

For a moment I couldn't move, and as the line of tears unraveled from my mother's eyes, I knew that I had no choice.

"Richie hates you," I said. "And so do I."

She groaned stupidly and I put the gun against the base of her skull and was about to close my eyes when my father appeared before me. I saw determination in his face and a bedside lamp high over his head. Shifting the Beretta to him, I fired again and again and again. He toppled sideways against the wall, the lamp bobbing forward. The bulb crashed against the hardwood floor and the thick iron base smacked my mother's skull. She stopped groaning instantly.

A few feet away, my father lay in a fetal position, his blue shirt and striped tie so covered with blood that I didn't know where the actual wounds were. His limbs twitched, but that didn't stop him from reaching out and groping at me.

When I fired the shot that killed my father, the ringing in my ears was so loud I couldn't hear a thing, not even the sound of my own screams. I slumped down against the wall and pulled my arms around my knees. I shivered and sat like that for minutes, closing my eyes, trying to block out the images that flashed inside my brain like slides.

I finally stood and dragged my parents' bodies into their bedroom one at a time, laying them beside their bed. Then I stumbled into the bathroom, stepping into the shower with my clothes still on. After a few minutes I peeled off my shirt and pants. The water that rolled off me was pink and so was my skin when I finished scrubbing it.

I lay down in my bed and pulled the blankets up to my chin, ignoring the wind's whistle from outside. I was almost sure I'd lie awake all night, but I was wrong. One minute I was staring bleary-eyed at the ceiling and the next thing I knew, pale yellow light streamed across the bed. It was morning.

New York State Police
interview with Travis Ellroy

DET. UPSHAW: I'm going to ask you again, why did you shoot
your parents?

TRAVIS: I don't know what you're talking about.

DET. UPSHAW: You don't know why you shot them?

TRAVIS: They're not dead.

DET. UPSHAW: You were at the funeral. Do you
remember that?

TRAVIS: Of course not. They don't have funerals for people
who're still alive.

DET. UPSHAW: We've discussed this already, Travis. The U.S.
marshals brought you to the cemetery in handcuffs.
There were a lot of TV cameras, I could even show you the
tapes. (SOUND OF PAPER SHUFFLING) Your parents were buried
right next to your brother. Don't you remember that?

TRAVIS: You're just trying to screw around with me, and it's
not going to work. I'm not buying it.

DET. UPSHAW: What about the next morning? After you
killed your parents?

TRAVIS: I didn't kill anyone.

DET. UPSHAW: When you went to school that morning,
what happened?

TRAVIS: I ... what morning are you talking about?

DET. UPSHAW: Okay, let's try something different. Why are
you here? In prison?

TRAVIS: I'm not answering any more questions, all right.

DET. UPSHAW: You must've done something, don't you think?
They don't put people in prison for no reason.

TRAVIS: I don't know. You're just ... you're trying to

confuse me. Besides, if you already know so much, what do you need me for?

DET. UPSHAW: I know what happened, Travis. I know the trajectory of every bullet, and I know where every one of them landed. But what I still don't know is why. Why'd you do it? (SILENCE, THEN END OF TAPE)

1 HOUR TO GO

BACK WHEN I WAS IN SEVENTH GRADE,
Richie came home one night, a Wednesday night, and said he was
dropping out of college. He'd only been at Syracuse University for
two and a half months, but it wasn't what he'd expected, especially
the football program. In high school he'd been able to dominate but
now the players were bigger, stronger, smarter. The coach told him
he'd been cut from the team and that was the last straw. He was leaving for good.

My mom and dad were worried after Richie moved back home,
but they were sure he'd snap out of his funk. This was Richie Ellroy
after all, the golden boy who'd succeeded at everything he'd ever
tried. Maybe going to Syracuse hadn't worked out, but something
else would.

This time was different though. Richie didn't have a job, so he
slept all day and went out at night with his old classmates. These
weren't his friends, who were away at college themselves, but the
guys who didn't go to school and spent all their money on six-packs.
My parents didn't like him hanging around with "those losers," but
there wasn't anything they could do. My dad wanted to give Richie
an ultimatum, tell him to enroll in school again or else, but my mom
wouldn't let him. She said he just needed time.

After a while Richie let his hair grow long and only showered
every other day at most. He wasn't around much but whenever he
was he ignored me.

The only time he seemed happy was on the weekends or breaks
when Beth came home from school at Binghamton. That summer,
when they were together again, he almost returned to normal. He cut

his hair real short and stopped seeing his drinking buddies and even talked about college again. You see, my mother kept saying, I knew it all along. But then Beth left for school and Richie was angrier than ever, not even waiting until it got dark to go get wasted.

"That's it," my father roared one night, after Richie had brought home some girl who giggled so loud she woke us all up. The girl had left, sobbing, when my father called her a slut. Then he turned his fury on my brother. "You've got to turn yourself around, Richard."

"Oh, stop," my mother said.

"No, you stop. Stop defending him, stop making excuses for him." My father pointed at Richie. "I know you've had some disappointments in life—well, who hasn't? I'm giving you until your birthday to get a job and get your shit together, otherwise you're out of here."

Richie said nothing and stormed into his room, slamming the door behind him. I was stunned. I'd never seen anything like this between Richie and my parents.

The night before Richie's birthday, I spent almost half an hour wrapping his present, the World's Greatest Brother trophy. He hadn't lived up to that title in a long time, but I wanted him to know that even if he was a college dropout, even if he wasn't playing football, he was still the person I admired most. He was my big brother.

I had just finished wrapping the trophy box when the phone rang. A few minutes later, I heard shouting through the wall. Richie yelled Beth's name a few times and then let out a long string of curses. I didn't know if he was still on the phone or not.

I hid the present under my bed and sat on the floor with a puzzle I'd been working on. It was supposed to be Alcatraz, but all I had so far was a patch of blue water and some worn gray stone. When I looked up, I was surprised to see Richie standing over me.

"I'm going to tell you one thing, Travis," he said, "and if you only ever do this one thing, then you'll be okay."

He sounded like he'd been drinking, but there was a strange clarity to his words. I looked back at my puzzle. There was a gray piece that seemed to belong to the stone, but I couldn't make it fit.

"Don't ever be a loser like me," he said.

I searched his face to see if he was kidding. A loser? Even after everything he'd been through, he was no loser to me. I still believed what my mother kept saying: Richie would pull himself together, Richie would be everything he'd always been and more.

As if to prove it, Richie plucked one piece out of my pile. It was the lower half of a barred window and he slid it right into place. But instead of being grateful, I was angry.

"I can do it myself," I snapped, and Richie pulled back as though he'd been bitten.

"I know you can, little brother." He smiled, looking even more sad than before, and walked out.

"Hey, Richie, I've got something for you," I said, grabbing his present, but he must not have heard me. His footsteps drifted down the hall. The front door slammed. He was gone.

That night I dreamed of Richie and I driving out on the open road, just the two of us, as he said, "Thanks for the trophy, Trav-oh. It's the best gift anyone ever gave me." The dream felt so real that I thought I was awake until the sound of the phone woke me up.

After the ringing stopped, the next thing I heard was my mother screaming. I pushed into my parents' room and looked at her, the phone clutched to her chest. The bedside clock read 12:42 A.M., meaning it was forty minutes into Richie's birthday. "Who is it?" I asked, but my mother never answered. She couldn't.

It was my father who told me Richie's body had been found by the bleachers at Shadwell High, his old .22 rifle at his side.

• • •

When I woke up on what would have been Richie's twenty-fourth birthday, I had forgotten so much—from Richie's suicide to my parents' murder and everything in between—that my body felt light with happiness. But then I saw the comic books I'd swiped from Daniel's room on my bed, and the sight of them jolted me back to reality.

I hadn't eaten since the previous morning, and my stomach was practically roaring. To make it to the kitchen, I had to go through the bloody hallway. The door to my parents' room was closed, but I knew what was on the other side. Sort of, anyway. I remembered that I'd shot them, but I couldn't remember exactly how it had all played out.

All through breakfast something didn't feel right to me, and it wasn't just my mother and father being dead or the black hole in my memory. Whatever it was, it didn't hurt my appetite. I toasted two frozen waffles, ate them with lots of syrup, and then I had two more, along with a cup of yogurt and a bowl of Cheerios. When I was done I left the dirty dishes on the table.

There was a bullet hole in Richie's door about the size of a little boy's fist. I got a couple of fingers through there and twisted the lock. Inside, someone had put everything back the way it was before Daniel and I had gone in there.

I pushed past the clothes in the closet, including the football uniform which was now safely back inside its plastic wrapper. I found Richie's old Mongoose bike way in the back and wheeled it out. There wasn't enough air in the tires, but I found a pump on the closet shelf.

With the bike ready to ride, I rolled it into the kitchen. Then I went back and dug out the trophy I'd never had the chance to give

Richie. I wasn't sure why, but I put it in my backpack. Again, I felt that sense of strangeness, as though something about me was different, but I just couldn't place it.

I refilled the Beretta's magazine and slid the rest of the box of bullets into my jacket pocket. When I looked at the clock, I saw that it was already nine o'clock. I was late for school.

When I rode up to the bleachers and put the gun in my mouth, I only intended to hurt myself. I wanted to wipe out all the pain and confusion and desire with a single bullet. But I couldn't do it, and looking back, maybe a part of me had always known that. Why else would I have loaded all those slugs? Why else would I have gone back into my bedroom and put Daniel's comic books, the stolen yearbook, and the root beer can into my backpack? Why else would I have whispered "I'm sorry, I'm so sorry" as I left Richie's bike by the bleachers and walked into school?

My sneakers squeaked on the floor, and I waited for my eyes to adjust to the dim hall light. Someone came toward me and I tensed, barely able to make out the person's face. It was Taffy. She wore a V-neck sweater that showed plenty of cleavage. I stared at the tops of her breasts, daring her to say something, but she didn't. I thought again of how she'd hugged me in the vet's office when Simms was dying and I said what I'd wanted to say for years.

"Thank you."

She looked at me as though she wasn't sure what I meant. But she said, "You're welcome."

"I've got to go," I said.

"Guess you're late, huh?"

"Oh no, I'm not late," I said to Taffy. "I'm right on time."

Taffy scowled at me and turned, hurrying away. As she disappeared into one of the classrooms, I felt giddy. There were closed doors all along the hall and I knew that I could open any one I wanted. Instead I headed upstairs.

The sound of my sneakers echoed in the narrow stairwell. A small headache pressed against my forehead. I willed it away.

When I reached Mrs. Saxon's room, I stood on my tiptoes, pressing my face to the square of glass set into her door. P.J. was back today, moving his pen in lazy circles across his notebook. Jordan wrote busily. Mrs. Saxon stood in the middle of the room, her body hidden in a loose-fitting dress, navy blue with lace along the bottom. It was almost pretty.

My seat and Daniel's were too far back to see from this angle. Although Koryn's spot was closer to the front, Mrs. Saxon blocked my view of her. I waited, feeling the pressure in my calves as I stayed on tiptoe. After a few seconds, someone turned, pointed, whispered. I pulled up my backpack, feeling for the zipper, as Mrs. Saxon crossed to the board. Now I could see Koryn's desk. It was empty.

I dropped back on my heels and turned from the door, even as I heard it open. "Mr. Ellroy, are you just going to watch or do you plan to join us this morning?"

I said nothing. I expected to hear the voice then, and that's when I realized what had been bothering me: the voice was gone. I was pretty sure that I hadn't heard it since sometime the night before, during the episode with my parents. I missed it and wanted to bring it back, but I also knew that I'd never really been able to control it. It would show up again only if it wanted to.

"My name is Travis, you cow," I said, yanking the zipper on my backpack. I took a step toward the room and saw through the open doorway that Koryn wasn't the only one who was absent. Daniel's desk was empty too.

Mrs. Saxon just looked at me. She didn't know what I had in the bag, but she saw something change in my face, the way a jack-o'-lantern changes when you put a candle inside.

"Where are they?" I asked.

"Where's who?"

I went in the room and slammed the door behind us, holding up the gun for everyone to see. There was silence like I'd never heard before, not even during a big test. There was no sound of pencils scratching or feet tapping or bodies squirming. There was nothing.

"Koryn and Daniel," I said. "They're not here."

Mrs. Saxon backed away from me. As she bumped into her desk, her copy of *Wuthering Heights* flopped onto the floor. "What are you doing?"

"Why aren't they here?"

"Put that down, Travis. You're frightening me. You're frightening everyone."

It was true. My classmates' mouths were drawn into narrow lines, their eyes wide. Missy Relling squeezed her pencil and Lee Kartinski gripped the edge of his desk. Sean Delaney and Tiffany Erstad looked stone cold sober for the first time since fifth grade. Even P.J. was scared, his flesh drooping and lifeless without the anger that usually fueled him. But Jordan worried me the most. His hands were clenched over his notebook, his back rigid with fear, but I knew that his fear wasn't for him alone.

"Where is she?" I turned my eyes to Jordan, but kept the gun on Mrs. Saxon.

"Where's who?" he asked.

"You know who. Where is she?"

"She didn't come in today," he said.

"I don't believe you."

But Koryn's desk was deserted, no book bag or stray pencils beside it. I felt a prickly sensation in my stomach, the kind you get at the top of a roller coaster.

"Travis, why don't you put that, that thing down so we can talk." Mrs. Saxon's hands were shaking.

"The gun, Mrs. Saxon? Is that the 'thing' you mean?"

"Please, Travis. Please . . ."

"Just say it, Mrs. Saxon. Gun. It's just a word. There's no danger in words. Words can't hurt people. You're an English teacher, you ought to know that."

"Now, Travis—"

"Say it, Mrs. Saxon. Today's word is *gun.*"

"Oh no, Travis, please—"

Her words were cut off by an explosion that was quick and sharp and fierce. The bullet cut through her dress, opening a jagged red hole in her flesh. She collapsed on the floor, back against her chair, legs splayed in front of her, blood spreading around her body the way the syrup had spread on my plate of waffles. Her mouth moved, but she didn't make a sound.

Now the class was *really* scared. They scrambled under their desks, flattening their bodies against the floor.

"Nobody move," I said.

Most of them listened, but not P.J. He backed away to the window, using both of his hamlike arms to try to lift it. It only rose an inch or two, even with the full force of his strength. Several students looked at him, perhaps weighing their own chances of getting out with him.

"Now someone's going to tell me where Koryn is," I said.

Jordan lay flat against the floor, his fingers spread on either side of his face. I aimed the gun at him, while P.J. continued to struggle with the window. Mrs. Saxon lay silently, blood erupting from the hole in her chest.

"I already told you, she's out sick," Jordan said.

"Don't hurt us, Travis. Please." This was from Missy Relling, who crouched under her desk, her face almost as red as her hair.

"Shut up. Now I won't hurt anyone as long as I find out what I want to know."

I didn't have much time. Already I heard movement in the hall, people who'd wandered out of their rooms to see what the loud noise had been.

I squinted down the Beretta's sight at P.J. He wrestled the window up another couple of inches. "Travis," he said, "I'll tell you where she is, but you've got to leave me alone."

"Fine."

From below, Jordan roared: "P.J., goddamn it!"

P.J. glanced at me, his chest puffing out as he said, "She's in the principal's office, Daniel too, they're having some kind of powwow. About you."

"He's lying," Jordan said, but we both knew better.

P.J. had gotten the window up about two feet and stuck one leg over the sill, and in another moment or two he might've made his way out. But I wasn't going to let that happen. Just as I pulled the trigger, however, Missy Relling stood up and turned to the window, probably to join P.J., only the bullet caught her in the neck and knocked her sideways. She crumpled near Lee Kartinski's desk and he rolled away from her, whimpering.

There were several gasps. I saw faces pressed against the door's glass window, trying to see in. I imagined the word beginning to spread across the third floor like some high-stakes game of telephone: Travis has really gone off the deep end this time.

At the window, P.J. dragged his other leg across the sill, but he couldn't fit all the way through the frame. His legs dangled over the edge, his midsection caught. Drops of Missy's blood had landed on his face.

"You fat shit," I said, aiming the gun at him again, and a dark stain appeared at the crotch of his baggy jeans.

"Travis, don't," he whined.

I smiled and said, "Maybe you should've worn diapers, huh?" then squeezed the trigger twice. The first bullet burrowed into his side and the second caught one of his thrashing legs. Through the door behind me, I heard more activity in the hall, a buzz of voices, a herd of footsteps.

As I turned Jordan lunged at me in a crouch, wielding Mrs. Saxon's yardstick like a javelin. I fired at him. He fell and the ruler clattered to the floor. There was no time to check whether I'd hit him or not. I turned, shoved the gun in my backpack, and flung open the door, stepping out into the chaos of the hallway.

Dear Koryn,

The last day or so I've been thinking about what you said. I don't want to push you into anything you don't want to do. I don't want to hurt you, either.

So if leaving you alone is the right thing to do, I'll do it. Only I don't think it is, for you or for me. Whatever happened to you this summer, that's different. We're different. And the difference is I've never felt this way about anyone. Ever.

It's crazy to say this, now of all times. But I think I love you. I'm not even sure what that means, but I know it's true.

I'll probably tear up this letter in the morning. What else am I going to do with it? Go to school early, put it in your locker, hope you read it and understand?

I'd be too embarrassed for that. Too scared. But I want you to know that I'm here. And I'm not going anywhere without you.

Jordan

P.S. For the last stop on our trip, what do you think about Malibu, California? Have you ever seen pictures of it? The colors are so amazing. They practically hurt your eyes. Blue sky, white sand, green palm trees. Then at sunset, everything's orange and red. Even the ocean. I wonder what the waves look like in the dark. Don't you?

NOW

THE HALL WAS MOBBED. It was like class had just let out, only a hundred times worse. People were pushing and shouting and shoving, and suddenly I was terrified. Amy was in the midst of the mob, trying to claw her way past the crowd. I was tempted to shoot Amy but how could I? I couldn't kill everyone here, and even if I could, that wouldn't get me any closer to the people I wanted most.

As a clump of terrified freshmen scampered for the nearest staircase, I went past them, hearing cries of, "Watch out! He's got a gun! He's got a gun!" I just kept running for the other stairs.

All the doors on either side of the hall were open and through them I saw desks covered with notebooks and uncapped pens. Everyone was getting out fast, or trying to. I hung a left and when I got to the other end of the hall, there was a logjam of students squeezing into the stairwell, one of them shouting, "Move it, you assholes!"

I held my backpack against my chest as I joined the mob, and then I heard someone say "Travis!" Moira's round face bobbed up, and she let a couple of students surge past her so that I could catch up. When I did, she said, "Someone's got a gun." For an instant, I thought she was kidding, and then I realized: she had no idea it was me. Neither did anyone else at this end of the building.

She and I were carried in the crush of students, choked by the smell of animal fear and lemon polish. I saw Dana La Bret ahead of us, gobs of makeup streaming from her eyes. Finally Moira and I took the final steps to the ground floor.

As we got there, the fire alarm began to squawk, its bell clanging in my skull. The principal's office was to our right, the side exit to our left. Moira followed the rush of students past the library to the side door. I hung back, watching her go.

Dana crashed outside and a blast of cold air wafted back. The sound of ringing grew louder and louder as Moira forced her way ahead, and it was only when she put up a hand to hold the door for me that she realized I wasn't there. Laurel Zito, Koryn's friend, raced past her without looking back.

"Travis!" I had to read Moira's lips to know what she said. Her sudden look of anguish told me that she knew what I had done. Maybe she'd known all along but had hoped it wasn't true. Even now, she waited as other people pushed by, as if willing me to join her, but then Ross appeared behind her. He pulled her by the wrist, his eyes full of terror, and then my friends were gone. The door swung shut behind them.

Even as people continued to stream out, students and teachers jumbled together, I started in the opposite direction, back to the principal's office. I was just in time. Principal McCarthy ushered Beth, Koryn, and Daniel out into the hall ahead of him. Koryn and Daniel were so focused on getting away that they didn't see me. But Beth turned and her mouth pulled up as if she were trying to smile despite a shot of novocaine.

"Travis," she shouted. "What's going on?"

I didn't answer. Instead, I grabbed the Beretta from my backpack and fired at Principal McCarthy as he spun away from the door. He kept spinning, like a top gone out of control. The blood sprayed out of a hole three inches from his ear, redness striking the walls. Even as he collapsed he raised one hand, as if to bring it to his lips and whisper "Shhh," the way he did in the library. The hand dropped halfway to his mouth and flopped against his chest. He fell like a sack of laundry.

With me in the middle of the hall, Daniel, Koryn, and Beth

couldn't reach either exit, so they all ran to the cafeteria. I settled my aim between them and let off two quick but sloppy shots. Beth dropped to her knees, covering her head, while Koryn just froze, but Daniel kept running. I tried to get him in my sights but he zigzagged, pinballing between lockers. I let out a flurry of shots, three in a row. One clipped his upper thigh, his legs going out from under him.

As he fell, I dropped my backpack and shouted, "Freeze!" Racing ahead, I turned the Beretta on Koryn, who had curled up against the wall. She wore the tiger print shirt I'd seen her holding up in the mall the night Daniel stole the comic book.

"Stand up," I told her, shouting to be heard. "And put your hands out in front where I can see them."

Koryn put her hands out and Beth stood up beside her. She had a stubborn twitch in the side of her face, her low heels rooted to the floor. Daniel lay on his side a couple of yards past them. His eyes were closed and his chest rose gently as blood dribbled from his leg. He looked unconscious.

"Travis, let Koryn and Daniel go," Beth said. We were far enough from the bell that I could actually hear her.

"Why should I listen to you, you traitor?"

"Please, Travis," Koryn said. Strands of loose blue hair hung in her face.

I looked from her to Daniel. He seemed to be a few inches closer to the cafeteria than before, but I wasn't sure. Except for me, Daniel, Koryn, and Beth, the hall was empty.

"Travis, we're scared!" Beth yelled. "But we know you don't want to hurt anyone else."

"You've got no idea what I want."

I looked back at Daniel and this time I saw a streak of blood beside his leg. He had definitely moved toward the cafeteria. "Stay where you are," I snapped.

"All right," Beth said. "We're staying."

I stopped three feet from Beth and Koryn. Daniel was further along the hall. I stretched my arms out so that his head appeared over the sights like a lollipop. "You scheming son of a bitch," I wailed, "I'll piss in your guts and wipe my ass with your face and I'll make you pay!"

I was about to pull the trigger when I felt a weight around my midsection. Thick arms curled around me like a giant boomerang, and I toppled into the lockers. My head slammed into a metal grate, hot pain searing my scalp. I turned and finally got a look at my attacker.

It was Jordan.

I focused on trying to hold on to the Beretta, even as his fingers clawed at me, nails digging into my arms. "Run!" he shouted, but Koryn stood frozen, a perfect target. I fired and fired again but neither shot was close.

Daniel stood, a little groggy. Beth grabbed Koryn by the hand. Jordan turned back to me and kicked at my wrist, the gun skittering across the floor. He brought his foot back again, but as his sneaker arced in I grabbed his ankle.

Beth and Koryn ran toward the cafeteria. So did Daniel, who was back on his feet and running with only the slightest hint of a limp.

I ignored the three of them, sinking my teeth into Jordan's calf, biting through his socks, tasting old cotton and fresh blood. He shook his leg hard enough to loosen my teeth and I let go, shoving him. And just like that, it happened.

He fell on his right knee, his face tilting back, lower lip turned inside out. Ten months after being carried off the football field on a stretcher, he'd ruined his knee again. He screamed, chin dropping to his chest.

Daniel kept running at nearly top speed, but Koryn made a sudden about-face, crying, "Jordan!" Beth stopped and considered and kicked off her shoes, then started chasing after Koryn instead of following Daniel.

I ran for the gun with long, leaping strides, nearly losing my balance in a puddle of blood. As I reached for the Beretta, Jordan popped up beside me, his face twisted in pain. He grabbed my jacket pocket and when I spun, the pocket tore open, the box of bullets falling out, but at least I was free and the gun was right there. I closed my fingers around the Beretta but so did Jordan and there was Koryn, almost to us, and Daniel had limped to within about ten feet of the cafeteria, and if I could just get control of—

BLAM!

The sound of this bullet was louder than the rest, the force of it knocking me one way and Jordan the other. Dust puffed from the ceiling. I thought the bullet had gone straight in, but then I realized the slug had torn through Jordan first. He fell back, blood jetting out of his throat, the piece of my ripped pocket drifting from his right hand. His lips moved too quick, as though he was trying to spit out a lifetime of prayers in a few seconds.

"Jordan, no!" Koryn yelled.

Beth and Koryn were only two or three doorways away from us. Daniel was much further, only inches from the cafeteria. He might've disappeared inside if I hadn't pointed the gun at him and said, "Freeze."

He did.

Koryn held Jordan's face in her hands, crying. "Oh Jordan, I'm sorry, I'm so sorry for everything," she said. "Hold on! Please, just hold on! Oh God, oh God, I'll see you in Malibu. I promise, okay?"

Jordan quivered once and then was still except for the flap of burnt skin at his throat. An awful shriek rose from Koryn's lips. She looked ready to collapse, but Beth lifted her under the armpits, hauling her up with a strength I never knew she had.

Daniel remained caught in the Beretta's sights. He was about as far as I'd been from the cans during target practice, so he knew this was a shot I could make. Someone was going to get away from me, and I had to make a choice.

Sobbing, Koryn let herself be carried along by Beth, stumbling at first, legs unsteady. Beth's panty-hosed feet slipped on the blood and her skirt had pulled up so that I saw her black panties. I'd only had my eye on her for maybe a second or two but that was long enough for Daniel to try to duck through the doorway into the cafeteria kitchen.

I made a sudden turn, just the way we had practiced in the woods, the gun whipping around half a second before my body. I fired once, knowing my aim had to be perfect, and it was. Blood rifled out of Daniel's shirt as he fell.

I ran toward him, careful not to step on the spilled bullets or the empty casings, knowing that behind me, Koryn and Beth would be almost to the side exit by now. I wanted to shout after them, to tell them that I was glad they were the ones to get away, but I had to get to Daniel and finish what I'd started.

Suddenly the fire alarm cut out, the silence as deafening as the noise had been. It felt like Daniel and I were the only people in the whole world as he lay there, blood squirting out between his fingers.

"You won't shoot me," he said weakly.

"I've already done it twice," I said.

He coughed a couple of times and I half expected to see more blood on his lips. "After everything I've done for you?"

"You didn't do shit for me. You lied to me, you treated me like crap, you made a fool out of me. And now you're going to get your payback."

From outside, I heard sirens, faint at first but growing louder and louder.

"I was trying to help you," Daniel croaked.

"Liar."

"It's true," he said, squeezing his eyes shut, as though wracked by sudden pain. "When the police get here, you're finished."

"Don't you mean *we're* finished?"

"Me? I didn't do anything, Travis."

"You told me to do this. You wanted this."

"I'm not sure if the police will see it that way. 'No, officer, I had no idea what Travis was going to do. But he was very unstable. I can't really say I was surprised, he was always a little off-balance.' "

"You're a liar."

"You're going away, Travis. For a long time. Or maybe not so long. They have lethal injection in this state, you know. Or you could just do it yourself, put yourself out of your misery. Just pull a Richie Ellroy and blow your brains out."

I looked at the gun and then at him. Despite all the lies, a part of me thought I'd be friends with Daniel forever and he would always be at my side. But I saw for the first time how much I was truly alone. My brother was gone, my friends too, and Daniel was right, there was only one thing to do.

I put the gun between my lips, its barrel shockingly warm against the roof of my mouth, and set my finger against the trigger. Outside, on the bleachers, I hadn't had the guts but this was different, because the only way to teach Daniel a lesson was to make him see what he had done to me.

"Here you go, Richie," I shouted, even though I meant Daniel, and pulled the trigger.

I braced myself for the sound of the shot, but there was nothing, not even a whisper. The Beretta was empty.

When I first started to pull the trigger, the corners of Daniel's mouth had turned up in a smile, his eyes shimmering like a lizard's scales in the sun. Now that the gun hadn't fired, there was a sudden narrowing of his eyes and the collapse of his smile, and then that too was gone, replaced by a blankness that was like Mrs. Saxon's blackboard on the first day of school. I thought again of seeing Daniel in the mirror in Richie's room, when I'd tried on the football uniform, and I knew then that *this* was his true face. This emptiness, this coldness. Everything else was just a mask he covered it with.

"Shit," he said.

And I laughed. What else could I do? Daniel shook his head and put his hands out, wincing a little as he stood, but once he got to his feet he looked okay. Outside, the sirens shrieked like babies on the maternity ward.

"I shot you," I said, watching the blood bubble out of his side.

"Grazed me, really." He touched his fingers to the hole in his shirt. "Flesh wound."

And then he started to walk away, like a cowboy at the end of an old western, only he was still limping a little, and I squeezed the trigger again and again, but it just made that same empty sound. Whirling, I ran after him and when he saw what I was doing he ran too. He was probably faster than me but the gunshot had slowed him enough so that I caught up to him about midway down the hall, right by Principal McCarthy's body.

I swung my forearm at Daniel's head and he stumbled. Then I shoved him against the wall and slammed a fist into his belly. He folded forward, gasping, and I swung again. But even as my arm came in I felt something sharp pierce my flesh and when my fist reached his gut again, there was no power left behind it.

Looking down, I saw a pool of red along my arm, blood pooling into my elbow. Daniel held his pocketknife in his hand, its blade glistening with red.

"Good-bye, Travis," he said, and walked away, facing me at first, the knife still drawn, but when I didn't follow he folded it up and turned away.

I went over to my backpack and dug into it for something to stop the bleeding. But all I found were memories: the sketch of Koryn, the drawing of Daniel under the desk, the root beer can, the comic books, the yearbook, Daniel's note from the first day. I flung these after Daniel with my good arm, the yearbook and comic book pages flapping, the can tinkling, the sketch paper drifting down like snow.

Finally I seized the World's Greatest Brother trophy, grabbing it by the top of the plastic figure and hurling it. It spun end over end, smashing into the floor a couple of feet from Daniel, but he didn't even flinch.

A moment later he started to run again, the blood from his leg leaving a trail like breadcrumbs in a fairy tale. He was so far away from me he had no reason to run and even less to cry out. "Help me! Somebody help me! Please!" Then I got it. This was just another performance, a show for the police officers outside.

As Daniel burst through the school's front door, the end of period bell bleated in the air above me, and I half expected the doors to fly open and students to flood the hall, but it was deserted except for some forgotten backpacks and blood. Hands shaking, I let the gun fall between my sneakers, which were streaked with blood from my arm. The bleeding had slowed but the wound started to throb.

The sirens were almost deafening as I went down to the side door and looked out through a smudged window. Students and teachers had clustered by the stone fence, Beth at their center. Another group was moving toward town. I could make out some of the faces, but just barely: Ross and Moira, Taffy and Amy. Koryn stood on the lawn, alone, and Daniel was running to the parking lot.

Again, I waited for the voice to speak up inside of me, and then

I realized it wasn't going to come back this time. It didn't have to. The moment I'd picked up that gun, the voice and I had become one, each inseparable from the other.

I stepped away from the door and I screamed, screamed for all the time I'd lost and for the empty gun and for everything I would never have, never know. I screamed but I did not cry.

Backing down the hall, I saw a brown paper lunch bag someone had dropped in all the confusion. I found the remains of a crushed tuna sandwich inside. I wondered what kind of food they'd have in prison and I ate the sandwich, even though it was soggy, so that I wouldn't be hungry when I got there.

ONE
YEAR LATER

IT'S AMAZING HOW FAST I got used to prison. At first I was in the Dutchess County jail, where I had a big empty cell and a plastic bed. I had to wear a paper gown and paper boots and my feet were always cold. After a couple of weeks, though, the county took me off suicide watch and I got a blue jumpsuit with matching blue sneakers and a metal bed just like everyone else.

In those days I had a lot of visitors. Different police officers kept coming, and there was also my court-appointed lawyer, Sebastian Toye. For a couple of weeks he brought me back and forth from court almost every day. Mr. Toye told me that it was best to try to arrange a plea bargain, otherwise the state would go for the death penalty. I told him that whatever he wanted to do was okay. When the judge finally accepted my guilty plea and asked if I understood what I was doing, I said, "Yes."

But I didn't understand, not really, because somehow I'd forgotten everything that happened in my last week or so on the outside. I knew there'd been some terrible tragedy and people blamed me for it. I was pretty sure that Daniel and I had done something together, something awful, only he wasn't in jail and I was.

I saw him in court one day, but he didn't look the way he used to. His hair had grown out and he had a fuzzy goatee that made his whole face look funny. He wore a pair of long johns with a T-shirt over it and a gold chain that glinted in the too-bright light of the courtroom.

Koryn was there too, though I almost didn't recognize her. Her hair was a single shade of blond and cropped at her shoulders. She wore makeup along her cheeks and eyes and lips, but most of it was ruined as soon as she started talking.

Ross and Moira looked about the same, though Moira had lost some weight and wasn't wearing a baggy sweater. Ross was still pale and quiet. When he was on the stand, the lawyer had to remind him to speak into the microphone. He and Moira barely looked at me, even when I waved and smiled.

My parents didn't bother to show up in court, but that was fine. I didn't need them. I didn't need anyone.

After sentencing I was moved from the county jail to Dannemore Penitentiary. DP was only about an hour or so north of Shadwell. I'd driven by it on the thruway once, when my parents and I took Richie up to school in Syracuse.

From what I'd seen in the movies and on TV, I'd always imagined prisons with huge barred doors and cold stone walls. But Dannemore is more like a hospital with its bright, white, shiny halls. The guards can be mean and even dangerous, but the other inmates are scarier than the guards.

In my first couple days I got beat up in the cafeteria twice, both times far worse than anything P.J. had ever done to me. But if you mind your own business, most guys will leave you alone. In that way I guess it's a lot like high school.

It's pretty lonely though. For months no one called or visited. At first I wrote letters to Daniel every day, but he never responded. Then, about five months after I got there, the guards told me I had a visitor. They didn't say Mr. Toye, who they all knew, and my heart began to beat very fast.

The small concrete room the guards led me into was filled by a man about as tall as my father but a little heavier. He had a thin horseshoe of blond hair and a ruddy face with a big nose. There was a small tape recorder and a black leather case on the table in front of him. He showed me his badge and introduced himself as Detective Carl Upshaw of the New York State Police. As he put the badge down, his coat hung open. His shoulder holster was empty.

"You don't have to be scared," Upshaw said.

"I'm not," I said.

"I should explain why I'm here. Over the last few months I've been conducting interviews about what happened in Shadwell. Talking to your old friends and teachers, trying to make some sense of everything. But there's so many missing pieces. I was hoping you could fill in the gaps."

"Did you talk to my parents yet?" I asked.

His eyebrows rose. "How would I do that?"

"I don't know, they've changed their number. You're a cop, though, so you've probably got some way to get the new one."

"I haven't talked to your parents. Do you know why not?"

"I guess you wanted to hear my side first."

"Do you understand what you've done, Travis?"

"Sure."

"Tell me." But I was silent. Detective Upshaw leaned forward, bracing his arms on either side of the tape recorder. "Do you think this is some kind of game, Travis?"

"No."

"Then you must know your parents are dead."

"That's not funny," I said, even as I felt the blood turning to slush in my veins.

"You're right, it's not." Detective Upshaw scratched at his nose with thin, hairless fingers. "Do you really think your parents are alive?"

"Of course they're alive," I said.

Upshaw proceeded to fire questions at me. He used the same tone of voice as the psychiatrists I'd seen, but he cared more about what I had done than about how I had felt doing it. Mostly I didn't know what he was talking about, and I told him so. But he kept asking the same questions again and again, just like Sheriff Riley after I threw those rocks. That, at least, I could remember.

"You're not faking, are you?" he said finally.

"What is this bullshit?"

"Just think, Travis. Take yourself back to that time last fall, the first day of school. What's the first thing you remember?"

"Nothing. I'm through talking about this."

"Do you remember meeting Daniel? He took your regular desk, didn't he? Is that how you started talking to him?"

I said nothing, and Upshaw didn't jump right into the silence the way most people did.

Finally he leaned forward, but he still wasn't close enough for me to reach him. "I'm no shrink, Travis, but I've taken some psychology courses. And here's one thing I know: you don't forget something as traumatic as this. You might bury it deep down inside, but it's there. If I could bring in an expert, someone who does hypnosis, maybe we could—"

"Forget it."

"Of course, the memories might just come back on their own, you know. With the right trigger."

"Why should I care what happened? Is it going to change anything, Detective?"

For the first time that day, Upshaw was speechless. He gathered the cassette recorder and the tapes and slid them into his pocket. "If you ever want to talk, the warden here knows how to reach me. You give me a call anytime. If not, I'll stop by in a couple months, maybe you'll feel more like talking then."

"I doubt it," I said.

"You know, Travis, a lot of people out there seem to think you're some kind of a monster. But I guess we know better, don't we?"

This time I was the one who didn't know what to say. Apparently neither did Upshaw, because he left without another word.

I wasn't quite the same after that. As I went through the routine of my new life, every day the same as the last, I felt somehow off-kilter. Maybe it was the time of year. Mostly I didn't know the day of the week and I surely didn't know the date. But from the colored leaves that blew across the yard, I knew it was fall and I'd heard someone mention September. And somehow I knew, just knew, when the guard came out to the yard that morning and tapped me on the shoulder exactly what day it was.

It was Richie's birthday.

"Phone call," the guard said.

"For me?"

He didn't answer, just turned and walked back to a gated door. We went inside and followed the long gray corridor that led to the kitchen. The air smelled of bacon and sweat.

There was a row of three payphones bolted to a concrete wall in an alcove outside the kitchen. A second guard waiting there handed me the receiver for the last phone. "It's your brother," he said.

A chill filled my jumpsuit.

"My brother's dead."

"Yeah, well, you might as well tell him yourself."

I reached for the receiver, the plastic earpiece warm against my face. "Who the hell is this?" I asked, but I knew.

"Hello, Travis," Daniel said.

"I thought you'd forgotten about me."

"Of course not. But I've had to be careful."

225

I had to remind myself to breathe. The sound of the open line was very loud in my ear.

"What do you want?" I asked.

"What do *you* want?" Daniel replied.

I was about to say that I didn't know, but that wasn't true. I wanted so much, and yet all I said was, "I want to know why. Why me?" I wasn't even sure what I was asking, and yet I knew that this would be the most important question I'd ever ask.

"It's easy, Travis. I knew what you were from the first day I met you. A loser, a wuss, a guy who was just waiting for someone to come along and tell him what to do. I wanted to see how far I could push you, how far you'd go. Of course even in my best-case scenario, I never thought it would come to this. You did everything I could think of and more! You weren't weak like that little pussy Paul Feezer. He buckled under pressure, Travis. He didn't have what it takes. He didn't have that killer instinct."

"So that's why you murdered Paul? Because he wouldn't do what you wanted?"

"Murder? Oh no. You have to understand, Paul was my friend. He was the only kid in school who'd pay any attention to me. But really, I hated him as much as everyone else. He was whiny and boring and just a complete spaz.

"I started telling Paul what I really thought of him, and more. I told him that he was a loser, a nobody. I showed him just how pathetic his life really was. Finally he begged me to stop, he pleaded, but I told him that I couldn't, it was for his own good.

"He started crying and screaming and, well, he just snapped. He told me he was going to tell my parents how I'd been treating him. I warned him that was a bad idea. We fought about it, and he ran off into the woods. He saw that frozen lake and must've decided he'd take the shortcut, going over it instead of around it, only when he ran out on the ice, he fell in . . . and by the time I found him, it was too late."

I could see the scene in my head, not the way Daniel had described it—the way it must have been. Paul Feezer looking up through the ice, his glasses floating on the water—no, he'd lost his glasses in the woods when he started running from Daniel, a couple hundred yards back. Maybe Daniel had pushed him in but more likely he'd fallen in by accident. As Daniel had said, Paul was a spaz, and he probably hit a soft patch on the ice. Daniel watched from a safe distance, the expression on his face as cold as the water, until Paul finally quit kicking and splashing. Then Daniel went for help. Or maybe it wasn't like that at all. Maybe Daniel had stood over Paul, holding his friend's face under the surface, feeling the drops of ice water as Paul struggled. Or maybe . . . but after all this time, who could say how it really happened?

"But why, Daniel? Why did you do . . . *this?*" I still didn't know what "this" was. But inside my brain, I felt pieces of memory shifting like the tectonic plates I'd once learned about in earth science.

"I didn't do anything, Travis. You did it. To Mrs. Saxon, to P.J., to Koryn and Jordan, to your parents, to yourself. You did it. Not me."

"But I would never . . . I just wanted you to be my friend."

"I *am* your friend, Travis. I'm the best friend you'll ever have. Because I'm the only one who knows, who understands. But even friends have to go their separate ways."

There was a long pause and for a moment I wondered if Daniel had hung up. When he finally spoke, his voice was quiet and his words were slow, as if he was choosing each one carefully.

"You taught me a lot, Travis. But I'm not in high school anymore. You can't get along in the real world if you act the way we used to. You've got to earn people's trust. You've got to make them like you. You've got to keep your true face hidden . . . until the world is ready for it."

"You're just going to do it all over again, aren't you?" I still didn't know what he'd done, but I sensed it beneath the skin of my thoughts: hate, murder, betrayal.

"I doubt it. Why let someone else have all the fun? The only trick is not ending up where you are, Travis. But for that you've got to be steady, and stable, and charming, and a hell of a lot smarter than everyone else around you. And most of all, you've got to be careful. Very, very careful." I imagined Daniel rubbing his frail goatee thoughtfully. "I'm having such a good time at college, Travis. I really wish you could be here."

"I want to know where you are," I said.

"I'll send you my new address, but it's hard for me to write. I'm very busy." From his end of the line, I heard a girl's voice say, "Dan, come on already."

"I'm coming," he told her, his voice sweet and measured. Then: "Good-bye, Travis."

A few minutes later, the guard brought me back to my cell. I could've had a few more minutes in the yard but I didn't care. I lay on my bunk and drew a picture of Daniel and I pointing guns at each other. But at the last moment, instead of attaching Daniel's face to his body, I drew the beady-eyed, closed-off face of the Collector. He was smiling. I wasn't.

After finishing the picture I went to sleep, and when I woke there were glimmerings in my brain, half-remembered images coming into focus. All that I had forgotten began to float behind my eyes, and suddenly I knew that I had something to say, a story pictures alone could not capture. I sat at the desk bolted to the wall beside my bunk, stared at a blank sheet of sketch paper, and began to write: *I rode my dead brother's bike down the concrete path that split the main lawn of Shadwell High* . . .

After that the words came quickly and so did the tears. I tried to stop them, but I couldn't. It was too late.